DIE LAUGHING

Longarm bellied up to the bar on the far side of Gluepants and Dallas with his back to the trio of well-dressed Mexicans, keeping an eye on them in the back-bar mirror from under his lowered hat brim.

Sure enough, as Gluepants told a bawdy joke about a lonesome sheepherder, the three swarthy strangers rose from their table and spread out, all three of them staring at the back of Longarm's denim jacket as one moved along the front window, another slid along the back wall, and the one in the middle just kept smiling sleepily as he drifted in.

Gluepants was saying, "In the morning as he counted his flock the old sheepherder says, 'One, two, three . . . good morning, darling . . . five, six . . .' What the hey?"

For Longarm had spun away from the bar with his gun drawn, shouting, "Hit the dirt!" in a loud tone of military command.

Then all hell broke loose.

TABOR EVANS

LONGARM

AND THE
UNWELCOME WOOLIES

JOVE BOOKS, NEW YORK

THE BERKLEY PUBLISHING GROUP
Published by the Penguin Group
Penguin Group (USA) Inc.
375 Hudson Street, New York, New York 10014, USA
Penguin Group (Canada), 10 Alcorn Avenue, Toronto, Ontario M4V 3B2, Canada
(a division of Pearson Penguin Canada Inc.)
Penguin Books Ltd., 80 Strand, London WC2R 0RL, England
Penguin Group Ireland, 25 St. Stephen's Green, Dublin 2, Ireland (a division of Penguin Books Ltd.)
Penguin Group (Australia), 250 Camberwell Road, Camberwell, Victoria 3124, Australia
(a division of Pearson Australia Group Pty. Ltd.)
Penguin Books India Pvt. Ltd., 11 Community Centre, Panchsheel Park, New Delhi—110 017, India
Penguin Group (NZ), Cnr. Airborne and Rosedale Roads, Albany, Auckland 1310, New Zealand
(a division of Pearson New Zealand Ltd.)
Penguin Books (South Africa) (Pty.) Ltd., 24 Sturdee Avenue, Rosebank, Johannesburg 2196,
South Africa

Penguin Books Ltd., Registered Offices: 80 Strand, London WC2R 0RL, England

This is a work of fiction. Names, characters, places, and incidents either are the product of the author's imagination or are used fictitiously, and any resemblance to actual persons, living or dead, business establishments, events, or locales is entirely coincidental.

LONGARM AND THE UNWELCOME WOOLIES

A Jove Book / published by arrangement with the author

PRINTING HISTORY
Jove edition / March 2005

Copyright © 2005 by The Berkley Publishing Group

ISBN: 0-515-13900-9

JOVE®
Jove Books are published by The Berkley Publishing Group,
a division of Penguin Group (USA) Inc.,
375 Hudson Street, New York, New York 10014.
JOVE is a registered trademark of Penguin Group (USA) Inc.
The "J" design is a trademark belonging to Penguin Group (USA) Inc.

PRINTED IN THE UNITED STATES OF AMERICA

10 9 8 7 6 5 4 3 2 1

Chapter 1

The jury had returned its guilty verdict in less than an hour and the firm but fair Judge Dickerson was smiling as he asked the accused if he had anything to say before the sentence was pronounced. After a soon-to-be-late Elmo Sawyer had rambled some about how sincerely sorry he was and promised he'd never do it again, the fair but firm Judge Dickerson was still smiling as he replied, "I believe you are sincerly sorry, and I know you will never do it again because it is the sentence of this court that you be hanged by the neck until you are sincerely dead. Case closed, and this court is adjourned for the day!"

So Deputy U.S. Marshal Custis Long of the Denver District Court was on his feet and out the door, hoping to make it to the back stairs of the federal building before anybody noticed his usual workday had over an hour and a half to go.

But his boss down the marble hall, Marshal Billy Vail, had seen it would be an open-and-shut case. So he'd positioned Henry, the young squirt who played the typewriter and kept the files for them, to block that escape route and herd Longarm, as their senior deputy was better known around the federal building, back to their office and through the same to the oak-paneled, smoke-filled inner

1

sanctum belonging to the formidable figure who signed all their pay vouchers.

As Longarm entered, lighting one of his own three-for-a-nickle smokes in self-defense, Billy Vail smiled knowingly from behind his cluttered desk and remarked, "I heard about the cake sale and hoedown out to the meeting grounds. It's a good thing Henry headed you off before you got a set-down shave and a haircut for nothing. I got to send you down to Albuquerque on a field mission that could last long as six weeks. Before you cloud up and rain all over me, it wasn't my grand notion. Bureau of Indian Affairs asked for you by name again. It's your own damn fault for getting along so well with cowboys, Indians and Mexicans, all of which we have in tedious abundance down New Mexico way at the moment."

There was only one chair and no ashtray at all on Longarm's side of the desk. Knowing Billy Vail had never seen fit to offer him a seat he sat down uninvited and, having mentioned the lack of ashtrays in the past—in vain—flicked the tip of his cheroot over the threadbare rug to let the ash fall wherever it felt best.

Vail frowned and growled, "Damn it, you untidy cuss!" But since he'd wearied of the game as well, Vail leaned back to take a deep drag on his own big black cigar as Longarm asked who they wanted him to arrest down New Mexico way.

Vail said, "Nobody, we hope. It all started out with good intentions. But the best-laid plans of mice, men and the Bureau of Indian Affairs gang aft agley. You wasn't out our way when Colonel Kit Carson rounded up the Navaho and frog marched 'em over to the Pecos back in '63, were you?"

Longarm soberly replied, "They had me tending other chores at a place called Chickamagua. But some Ute who were there with Carson told me about that campaign."

He blew a thoughtful smoke ring before he soberly added, "Some of the Ute seem to feel they were short-

2

changed after helping Kit Carson run their Navaho enemies out of the Canyon de Chelly."

The older and chunkier lawman shrugged and said, "My heart bleeds for the fucking Utes and all them white women they fucked up around White River in their own frisky way."

"Coloro's band wasn't the bunch who fought under Kit Carson," Longarm pointed out.

Vail said, "Whatever. The Ute are not the problem this season. The problem is the Mescalero off the reservation and the sincere desire on the part of both the army and the BIA that their Navaho cousins stay put!"

He let that sink in before he explained, "In their own wilder days up in the Four Corners, the Navaho raised just as much ned as any other so-called Apache, which means *enemy* in the Pueblo dialect. But after they got to weep by the waters of Babylon, or under the guns at Fort Sumner for five years, the ones who'd survived conditions in the black alkali swamps of the Bosque Redondo seemed willing to heed the advice of old William Tecumseh Sherman, who assured them war was hell and they hadn't seen the half of it if they ever started up with their Great Father again."

Longarm flicked more ash on the rug and wearily pointed out, "I have heard that tale from Navaho who tell it better. They were so glad their Great Father was letting them go home to the Four Corners that they took up new trades sincere, and they've been making out pretty good as silversmiths, sheepherders and rug weavers instead of raiders."

Vail nodded his bullet head to reply, "Most of 'em, least ways, but with no warfare to thin their ranks and even ugly Navaho gals having no trouble marrying up if they weave good blankets, the Navaho nation has been growing in numbers, with all too many in their teens, and the devil always having work for idle hands. So the army and the BIA both agree it would be best for all concerned if those young

3

bucks had more sheep to herd and sheer so's their kid sisters could be taught the weaving skills the nation has been getting famous for."

He exhaled a venomous cloud of cigar smoke and added, "Their blankets are getting popular as buffalo robes back East. Traders have tried to convince Navaho women to weave raw wool shipped in from other parts. But the superstitious gals are set in their ways. Seems they got to know a sheep personal before they'll card and spin its wool and, try as they may, the traders can't get Navaho weavers to try for neat and tidy. They say it's asking for trouble to weave a perfect Navaho rug."

Longarm nodded and said, "That's how you can tell a genuine Navaho rug from a machine-made fake. The real thing always has at least one mistake in the weaving, lest the sacred spirits think the weaving gal is showing off. They tell stories like the ancient Greeks told about that human gal who bragged her spinning was perfect and got turned into a spider by a pissed-off goddess."

He flicked more ash. "Seems to me I read somewhere how a white gal collecting Navaho rugs has started advising other collectors to look for that one small mistake in a genine Navaho rug.

"I read more than I likely should when I run low on pocket jingle before payday. Beats jacking off and you never know when some useless information you read might pan out useful."

Vail grimaced and replied, "I'm glad you know so much. Saves me talking a heap of shit about Navaho sheep. Suffice it to say they've been weaving all them wonderous blankets from the scanty wool of a scrawny critter called the charro breed."

Longarm shook his head and said, "Charro translates more like our word *mutt* than anything fancy as a *breed*."

Vail shrugged and said, "Call 'em charros or Great Horned Owls but your average Navaho is lucky to shear a pound of wool from 'em. And if you go to eat one they dress out at around fifteen pounds of mighty stringy mutton. So what can you tell me about the Spanish merino if you read so much?"

Longarm thought before he replied, "Sheepherding ain't my line but I do seem to recall the Spanish merino can live on marginal range and still yield a seven-pound fleece and mutton fit to eat."

Vail said, "That's what the BIA heard. So they've assembled a herd of six thousand prime merino ewes down Albuquerque way. The original plan was to drive 'em northwest to what's left of the Navaho reserves in the Four Corners county where Colorado, New Mexico, Arizona and Utah come to meet. The fresh stock is fertile. Mixing that many high-grade sheep in with them charros ought to upgrade the whole herd in no time and watching 'em do it was meant to distract 'em.

"When General Sherman advised the White House it was time to either wipe the Navaho out once and for all or give them a sporting chance on their original marginal range, it was already going on too late. The best grazing along the wetter eastern stretches of their original holdings had been claimed in their absence by white stockmen up from West Texas. They're still there. Holding a north-south strip around eighty miles wide betwixt the largely Mexican or Pueblo bottomlands of the upper Rio Grande and what is now the officious reservation of the Navaho Nation."

To which Longarm could only reply, "Ouch!"

Vail said, "It gets worse. Mex sheep outfits betwixt Albuquerque and Santa Fe were perfectly willing to sell sheep to the BIA or anyone else at the going price. So the BIA bought 'em. Six thousand head, like I said, all penned in and raring to go just outside of Albuquerque as they have to be fed and watered day by day at the going rate."

Longarm nodded and said, "Only no Mex is about to herd sheep across range claimed by cattlemen of the Tex persuasion. And inviting Navaho to just come and get 'em

5

would constitute an Indian uprising in the eyes of your average Texas cowboy."

The deputy marshal took a deep drag on his cheroot and asked, "You say they asked for me by name. What in blue blazes am I supposed to do about such a fix?"

To which Vail could only reply, "Beats the shit out of me. I know the advance party stuck in Albuquerque sent East for some braver but greener professional sheepherders. I suspect the plan is for you to somehow lead the way, keeping the greenhorns from getting struck by sidewinders or shot by good old boys who might be more impressed by your rep as an old cowhand with pals in the beef industry. I told you none of this was *my* grand notion. I don't see how you're going to do it, neither. So why don't you just go on down to Albuquerque and ask the rascals who asked for you? If you catch the five-thirty-five D and RG southbound you'll get into Albuquerque in the wee small hours and have time for a few winks before you meet up with the boss BIA dude, called Dodsworth, at the hotel Henry's booked you into. He might have something figured out. I know I don't."

Longarm swore under his breath and rose to his considerable height as he said, "He'd better. I'm coming back if he hasn't. I used to think I could walk on water until I almost drowned a few times. Trying to herd unwelcome woolies through eighty miles of cattle country could take a good fifty years off a man's life and wouldn't do the sheep a whole lot of good, neither!"

Vail just told him to manage as best he could. Longarm was still cursing as he stomped through the front office, grabbed the onion skins from old Henry and stuffed them in a side pocket of his tobacco-tweed frock coat.

Not wanting to miss that train and knowing he'd be meeting up with a bunch of Washington hands, Longarm didn't change from his dress-code three-piece suit and tie when he dropped by his furnished digs to pick up his McClellen and Winchester with the saddlebags packed for the road. He always kept faded but clean riding duds packed for the field. What President Hayes and Miss Lemonade Lucy (who wouldn't even serve soft liquor at the White House) would never know couldn't hurt them, once a federal rider was out on the open range a piece.

But if the truth were to be told, Longarm didn't look as citified as he imagined, toting his scuffed and heavily laden army saddle through the streets of Denver to the Union Station in his low-heeled army boots worn under far from fancy tweed pants. And more than one old soldier he passed noted the cavalry set of his pancaked black coffee Stetson and the double-action .44–40 Colt riding cross-draw under the left tails of his loose frock coat with its tailored grips peeking forward from time to time as he strode along.

The shoestring tie Longarm wore with his hickory work shirt was far from fancy and the gold washed watch chain across his tweed vest looked close to utilitarian even when you didn't know there was an accurate but inexpensive watch at one end and a double derringer at the other. In sum, men who worried about such things tended to guess the tall, tanned gent with gun-muzzle gray eyes and a heroic mustache was likely what he was: a lawman or a hired gun. Nobody who studied such matters tended to take him for a tinhorn gambler or a whisky drummer.

Once he'd checked his baggage through to Albuquerque Longarm stocked up on extra smokes, aware how prices rose once the candy butchers had a smoking man at their mercy aboard a moving train. He picked up a couple of magazines to read aboard the train as well. He'd already finished the *Illustrated Police Gazette* by the time the five thirty-five was rolling through the yards to the south and a conductor he didn't know was working his way along the car, punching tickets.

Longarm had a railroad pass, issued by the Denver & Rio Grande for past favors with unfortunate train robbers. But some sneaky small voice in the shadows of his mind whispered a half formed warning about a nosey-looking conductor. So he told the cuss he hadn't had time to pick up his ticket to Albuquerque in the station and paid the eight dollar fare like a sport, knowing he'd be able to charge it to his expense account back in Denver. He was still wondering why he'd done that when he ambled back to the club car, sprung another two bits for a schooner of suds and took it to an empty table near the rear of the car to nurse it as they got to rolling faster across greened-up range with the afternoon sun low above the purple peaks of the Front Range off to their west.

Had one of the conductors he knew been punching tickets Longarm might have bummed the use of an unbooked Pullman compartment off him. He knew the haul ahead was fixing to get tedious and he'd arrive gummy-eyed and dying for a flop around four in the morning. So how come that small voice kept telling him to tough it through?

He didn't know. He seldom did. But he'd learned to listen to such advice way back when they'd been holding that war in his honor. Indians he'd talked to had assured him it was medicine. Wild critters had such medicine as well. Folk who tried to reason with their medicine got to where they didn't listen to it, and not listening to your medicine could get you in all sorts of trouble.

He lit a smoke to help him nurse his beer as he absently admired the tall brunette with Anglo features and a border riding habit jawing with that same conductor at the far end of the club car's bar. The both of them were trying so hard not to glance his way that Longarm suspected they were talking about him. He knew he'd guessed right when the tall brunette carried her mint julep back to join him at his table, uninvited, and quietly asked, "Might you be the one they call Latigo Shaw?"

Longarm cautiously asked what might have made her think that. She said, "You fit the description Two Ton Tobin gave us and they just told me you were getting off with me

8

at Albuquerque. I'd be Judith Morrison. Two Ton would have told you about me, of course?"

Longarm soberly replied, "Of course," having no idea who she might be but knowing Latigo Shaw rode for the Wyoming Cattleman's Protective Association, while Two Ton Tobin was a cattle buyer with a sinister rep.

The brunette continued, "I was so worried when I missed you in Denver by hours. When they told me at the Tremont House you'd just checked out I hoped you might have gone south to see what might be keeping me. I guess Two Ton told you what we wanted from you, ah, Latigo."

Longarm risked replying, "Not in so many words, Miss Judith. Old Two Ton implied you'd fill me in, yourself."

She nodded and said, "*Bueno.* I'll get right down to brass tacks. We've gotten word a big sheep outfit is horning in on our range and we don't cotton to it one little bit. So we're offering a bounty of one dollar a sheep, a hundred dollars a sheepherder and five hundred for the son of a bitch leading the drive!"

Chapter 2

Longarm didn't laugh. You didn't laugh at a Texas funeral or fart in a Texas church, and it was an article of Texas faith that sheep and cattle could not be raised in the same state or territory.

He knew better than to tell any lady with a West Texas twang how they raised cows, goats and sheep on the same Mexican haciendas or grazed mixed herds of cattle and sheep on Australian range as dry as that of the American southwest. Neither he nor the U.S. Department of Agriculture was ever going to convince your average Texas cowhand that a sheep was not such a vile and stinky critter that a whalebone-tough Texas longhorn, who'd get by on sagebrush and tumbleweed if it had to and gobble cactus thorns and all, wouldn't shy away from freshly sprouted alfalfa if a sheep had passed anywhere near it. Any Anglo raised west of the Brazos knew a cow had to be protected from ferocious, all-devouring and likely rabid sheep—at gunpoint, if need be. Elephants were scared of mice, too.

The reasons for such firmly held religious notions on the part of Texas cattle folk, or others trained by Texas cattle folk, were twofold, with one reason more sensible than the other.

It was true sheep had front teeth, which cows lacked,

and thus could nibble closer where the range was over-stocked and poorly managed. In an eastern meadow or even on sensibly grazed western prairie, cattle and sheep grazed together efficient, with the cattle preferring the grass and the sheep browsing leafy forbs such as rabbit brush and dock to actually improve the chances of the western short-grass such as buffalo or grama.

But, of course, once crowded stock had overgrazed a stretch they all went after whatever was left and there a hungry sheep had the edge over a cow or any grazing critter with no front teeth. So range hogs feared more efficient grazers with good reason.

The less sensible but doubtless more emotional feelings about sheep in Texas cattle circles had derived of bitter Scottish history, Longarm had been assured.

Like Captain Ewen Cameron, who'd started the Texas beef industry with a herd of Hispano-Moorish longhorns he'd rounded up in Chihuahua during the Mexican War, a whole lot of Texas pioneers, starting with Jim Bowie, had been Scots, evicted from their Highland crofts in the early days of the industrial revolution to make room for the more profitable *sheep* the British textile industry favored. Highland crofters who'd worked the same land for hundreds of years were forced to leave forever by the Highland chiefs, and landlords, they'd fought and died for. Their houses had been torn down, their croplands plowed under and re-planted to pasture for bleating flocks of wall-eyed, dumb-ass, stinking, no-good *sheep*, and their wee bairns had been raised to feel as if it had been the sheep, not the selfish landlords, who'd driven them to an alien shore, to start all over, as vaqueros or buckaroos, if they were lucky enough to wind up in Texas where nobody but fucking greasers had anything to do with fucking *sheep*!

Only a modest percentage of Texas cowhands were of Scottish descent, of course. But the Irish, Dutch and such, who'd learned the skills of the buckaroo from the Scots who'd stolen them off the vaquero, believed what they'd been taught by the first non-Mexican whites who'd managed to make a good living west of where the cotton, corn and 'taters growed. So the West Texas Anglo followed ways that were in fact a blend of Hispano-Highland ways, good and bad, with the rooster strut of the Mex vaquero mixed with the prickly pride of the Highland clansman and a heap of just plain stubborn traditions you had to be from Texas to fully understand.

Being from a hardscrabble hill farm in West-by-God Virginia, Longarm had the advantages that came with having had to think for himself as a boy if he ever expected to grow up.

One of the things he'd learned, early on, was to keep his mouth shut and his ears open when he met up with folk more set in their ways. He'd found it worked with Mister Lo, the poor Indian, as well. Trying to tell a Mescalero or Navaho it was all right to eat fish was just another way for a white man to wind up dead and Agent Meeker, up to the White River Reservation, never should have tried to tell those Utes their best horse pasture made more sense as a potato field.

So instead of telling Judith Morrison she was *loco en la cabeza* and out to wind up in prison, Longarm told her, as Latigo Shaw, he aimed to scout that infernal sheep outfit before he shot anybody. He confided in a professional tone, "As our mutual friend, Two Ton, must have told you, I have a private detective license, issued lawful by a justice of the peace. So I got to follow certain rules lest I be taken for a common assassin. To begin with I would shoot a dozen sheepherders before I'd shoot one sheep. You can almost always justify taking a human life, but gunning *critters* can take you down a slippery slope called cruelty to animals."

She said, "Pooh, sheep are not animals. They're vermin. I'd as soon pet bugs as touch a stinky sheep!"

Longarm, in the guise of Latigo Shaw, gravely replied, "Me, too, but Mexicans sit on grand juries in this territory and some Mexicans nibble candied cockroaches. In the meantime, have you ever wondered how come you can get a year at hard-time in Colorado for abandoning a flock of sheep left in your care?"

She blinked and said, "No, I didn't know you could. How come?"

He said, "Cruelty to animals. Young jaspers signing on for a summer in the mountains herding sheep are forever suffering a change of heart and simply walking away from them and leaving them to shift for themselves."

He took a drag on his cheroot and explained, "Sheep don't shift for themselves worth mention in raw wilderness after thousands of years all domesticated. The ones the coyotes don't bring down tend to wander off cliffs or drown in whitewater they thought they could cross without the guidance of a keener mind. Ain't no need to worry about all those sheep if nobody herds them your way. See?"

He could see he'd got her to thinking. That had been his intent. You didn't convince a medicine man it was time to put aside his rattle and let you dose a fevered child with quinine. You admired the hell out of his fool rattle and asked if he'd ever noticed how his chanting enhanced the bitterness of the medicine dust you just happened to have brought along. Striking whilst the iron was hot, he said, "Here's my plan. When we get to Albuquerque we won't let enybody know I'm Latigo Shaw. I'll pretend I ain't working for you and your own. I'll pussyfoot my way into wherever that sheep outfit is forming up and ask 'em for a job so's I can spy on 'em and find out just what they might be up to."

She imperiously replied, "We already know what they're up to. Mexican riders who work *cows* have already told us they turned down work as sheepherders when it was offered to them by some coot called Dodsworth. You'd better shoot him first, no?"

As Latigo, Longarm shook his head and replied, "Not before I know who he is and what he's planning, in more detail. I once caught a man I was after in bed with his own wife and got away with it as a crime of passion. But I knew exactly what I was doing when I made things look as if I'd been out to save the poor gal he was in the act of murdering when I got there a split second too late."

She stared goggle-eyed at him and marveled, "You *do* have eyes as cold as Two Ton described them! Have you had supper yet? All this talk about blood and slaughter seems to have given me an appetite for a porterhouse steak cooked rare and they say the dining car up forward serves way nicer grub, eaten at a more civilized pace, than you can order off the trackside Harvey Houses if you go by way of the AT and SF."

He allowed he could go for steak and potatoes and felt curious about the French string beans they served on this line. So they finished their drinks and got to their feet, with Judith taking the lead as Longarm tagged along after her, admiring her rear view. He could tell she rode astride in those split leather skirts, as gals raised on cattle spreads were inclined to, no matter what Queen Victoria said. He warned the tingle he felt where *he* forked a bronc to simmer down. It was still broad-ass daylight outside and they were dammit on their way to supper.

The tall brunette with her own black Stetson hanging down her back on its braided leather kite string drew many an admiring glance from other men as she sashayed past in the coach cars ahead. Most of them looked away when they noticed what was following her. They passed through a forward Pullman car with its private compartments lined up to one side of the narrow companionway. Then they'd made it to the dining car and Longarm was surprised when his brunette guide suddenly crawfished back to collide with him, gasping, "Oh, my God, what's *she* doing aboard this train? Go back! Go back! We can't let her see us!"

So Longarm let go of her and took the lead as they headed back the way they'd just come. But before they could get far the gal behind him called out, "In here! Be

15

quick about it!" and he turned to see she had slid one compartment door open and was already moving through it.

So he followed and, once he had, Judith slid the door to the companionway shut, gasping, "Woosh! That was close! Set yourself down and make yourself comfortable while I dig into this picnic basket and see what I can manage for us!"

Longarm took off his hat and sat by the window on one of the facing green plush seats that made up into a single bunk bed once you had a mind to turn in. He knew from having ridden this line in the past how the bedding was stored overhead behind a panel that could fold down to become an overhead bunk as well. They hadn't tried to hide the wet sink built into one corner, but to use the shitter you had to lift what looked like the padded seat of a lonesome little chair. As Judith dug though a picnic basket perched atop her wardrobe trunk Longarm murmured, "Very nice. But weren't you planning on getting off at Albuquerque, Miss Judy?"

She said, "I was. The porter has orders to wake me up when we get as far as Bernalillo. I mean, what's money for if you expect a lady to be met at the station before dawn looking like something the cat dragged in? I see we've ham and cheese on rye with a thermos of coffee and a fifth of bourbon. Have you ever had Irish Coffee, Latigo?"

He was too polite to say he doubted hers would taste the same as they served it at O'Bannions by the Denver stockyards. Anything wet beat ham and cheese with nothing to wash it down.

As she built their drinks he asked her who they'd just fled in mortal terror. She said, "The Widow MacEwen off the Double W. She was one of the scaredy cats who voted against our taking up arms against that big sheep outfit. Lord knows what she was up to in Denver this afternoon. The point is that we don't want her and her faction to know I rode up there to get you and thank heavens caught up with you aboard this train. She has a lot of respect from the older members of our cattle crowd, in spite of being an old fuss who can't mind her own beeswax."

She handed him a thick sandwich and sat down beside him instead of across from him with both their drinks as she continued, "We told old Marmion MacEwen she was free to set out the dance and let the rest of us deal with the danger. She said I'd got too big for my britches since my Uncle Don died and left me the Rocking M. Try this Irish coffee on for size, Latigo."

He did; it was closer to the real thing than he'd expected. So he told her so. She dimpled at him in the tricky light and modestly observed, "I guess I know a thing or two about a thing or two. It was my idea to pass the hat when Two Ton Tobin said he felt our pain and knew a range detective who could make nesters, sheepherders and other pests run for their lives just by asking what they might be doing in Wyoming Territory. When I said we could use a man like you he said he'd wire you and set us up a meeting."

She washed down a healthy chaw with a heroic swig and Longarm had to wait a spell before she added, "When Two Ton told us you'd agreed to a meet up at the Tremont House in Denver, I was the one selected by our vigilance committee to meet you there and see if I could recruit you. I almost fainted dead away, right there in that hotel lobby, when they told me you'd been there two nights in a row and had checked out that very afternoon. I was afraid you'd wearied of waiting and gone on back to Cheyenne after I missed the earlier train we'd agreed I'd ride north."

She patted his knee, right friendly, and added, "But you were on your way south to see what could be keeping me and I *have* recruited you, have I not?"

When he truthfully allowed he wouldn't have been aboard that night train if he hadn't been somewhat interested in those mysterious sheep, she called him a darling man and swiveled on her shapely rump to kiss him full on the mouth. So he kissed her back.

17

French.

She pulled away with a startled gasp and demanded wherever he might have got the notion she was that kind of a gal. When he just smiled at her by the last golden rays of the sunset off to the west Judith laughed impishly, allowed they'd best go easy on that Irish coffee and drained her tumbler so she could spring up and build herself another.

Longarm knew the game she was playing. He hoped she hadn't guessed the game *he* was playing as he wondered where the real Latigo Shaw might be at the moment and how far he'd have to push this before he confided he'd found out that government herd was only on its way through new cattle country on its way to the old Navaho range that nobody else wanted. So he wasn't too concerned as to how their budding romance blossomed, or if it was going to blossom at all, and she, being a woman, wondered at the lack of anxiety she sensed as the sun kept going down. So she kept trying to warm him up, drinking faster and tonguing him deeper than she might have had he been sincerely desperate.

Thus it came to pass that as his practiced free hand slid up her firm horsewoman's thigh as if by invitation, she never asked where he thought it was going until she was trying to suck his tongue out by the roots whilst he explored her moist and quivering ring-dang-doo first with his teasing fingers and then with a raging erection as he pinned her trim derrier firmly to the floor with his own thrusting pelvis in the gathering dusk. It wasn't clear, at first, whether she was trying to wriggle out from under him, buck him off, or come ahead of him as she called him a brute or begged him to hump her harder. Her lips were locked against his whilst the steel wheels rumbled under them and the clickety-clack of the staggered rail lengths set a quick-step tempo to what she said he was doing to her. Finally, she gasped, "Oh, great day in the morning and

I'm really going to . . . Jesus! Yess! You really made me come and how did you ever *do* that, you freak of nature?"

To which Longarm could only modestly reply, "Practice. Would you like to make up the bunk bed so's we could rise from this fool floorboard and do things right, Miss Judith?"

Chapter 3

As Longarm folded the two seats into one bunk and covered the prickly plush with smooth bed linen, Judith coyly suggested he draw the green canvas window shades down. They were glad he had, later that night, when the train stopped for engine water and others got off to stretch their legs along the open platform by the light of a full moon whilst the two of them kept at it, hammer and tongs, atop the covers, naked as jays with her on top again.

He'd known right off, in spite of her flat stomach and firm young tits that put her somewhere on the comfortable side of thirty, that whatever she might be, an inexperianced virgin could hardly be it.

He was glad, in more than one way. For aside from it feeling so swell to his old organ grinder it left his conscience free to just take all she had to offer without any guilty aftertaste. He knew that unless she was a born actress lying like a rug she was enjoying herself as she went on wrapping him around her little finger with her love-slicked innards. Or so she thought. He'd given up arguing whenever she slyly suggested running the flock of sheep off the edge of a mesa, insisting it would be more a mercy killing than actual cruelty to the stinky flea-infested things.

21

He didn't see fit to inform her they called the wee beast-ies infesting sheep by the name of *keds*, which were a breed of blood-sucking wingless fly, if you were lucky. He suspected she'd be delighted to hear how the sheep could come down with the fatal louping-ill if you let 'em get in-fested with sheep ticks. Sheepherders who might not take a bath all summer ran their sheep through disinfectant dips every chance they got.

So the difference cattle folk said they smelled was more a matter of being less familiar than worse. He knew she didn't want to be told that. Nor how many big cattle outfits kept flocks around their headquarters spreads to furnish lamb, mutton or yarn for knitting or weaving linsey-woolsey which outlasted machine-made flannel by half.

He doubted she'd tell him where she'd learned to screw so fine if he just up and asked her. Her pillow talk was that she'd been brung up by a kindly uncle after her pa had run off and her ma had pined away as a ward of the state.

He knew the Widow MacEwen off the Double W would never know Judith Morrison liked to be on top unless they invited her to join them.

The notion inspired Longarm to ask just what that Widow MacEwen might look like.

The younger gal, who was gripping his semierection with her old ring-dang-doo, sniffed and said, "Poor old thing's close to forty in a summer frock and older in her work duds. Ropes and brands her own beef with her hands at roundup time. Wears lilac water and combs her hair of course, but she's let her hair get sun-bleached and her hide's tanned as an Indian's. You wouldn't fancy her, even if she still screwed men, which I doubt."

She moved experimentally and added, "Even if she did, she'd never give anything like this to you, Latigo. She spoke out against our hiring you. Said any man who'd gun another in cold blood for hard cash was a man no Christian had any business talking to. Said she'd set down to Sunday dinner with a small-poxed horse thief before she'd have

22

truck with a hired gun. I told her you were a licensed range detective but she told us a hired gun by any name would smell like a rotting corpse to her."

Longarm rolled the sass on her back to finish right in the image he'd just formed of an old gal he was commencing to admire. Roping Sally, up Montana way, had been a sun-bleached blonde who could rope and throw way better than most men by daylight and screw a man tender after dark. He'd bawled like a gal and hadn't tried to hide his tears when they had to bury what was left of old Roping Sally that time. So he shut his eyes and let himself go whilst for one brief magic moment he was back Montana way in a no-frills natural woman you didn't have to bullshit.

Of course, he'd no sooner come in Roping Sally's mighty pretty substitute before they were bullshitting one another some more. Playing it by ear, he was working on a plan to gain her confidence and then talk her and her wilder pals out of a range war by allowing he'd discovered, as a spy in their employment, that they might not want to kill a bunch of federal employees and draw the wrath of the U.S. Cavalry when they didn't really have to.

He could picture the good-old-boy guffaws when he told them on the sly those sheep they'd been so worried about were headed for the marginal range left to the Navaho instead of the better third of the old Navaho lands they'd been allowed to claim, improve and cherish.

Some know-it-all who believed in hoop snakes and the unusual private parts of Chinese women would likely object that six thousand sheep just passing upwind would ruin the appetites of their delicate longhorns. So he'd have to study some on those few in her bunch who seemed anxious to avoid trouble. If he and those BIA dudes could work out a corridor of uncontested passage across that wide strip of spanking new cattle range they could have the unwelcome woolies in Navaho hands within . . . how many risky days? You could drive cows twelve or more miles a day. How far could you herd infernal sheep? How come in all the time he'd been out this way he'd never asked because he'd never *given* a shit?

It surely beat all how, no matter how much useless-sounding information a man might bone up on, free, at the Denver Public Library, he was always stuck with new questions he'd just never asked.

He kissed the languid brunette and suggested they try for some shut-eye. She didn't argue. He'd established in another book from the medical stacks that no matter how they carried on, a woman was as anxious to sleep after a good piece of ass as any man. The reason so many women didn't just turn over and snore was that nine times out of ten the gal hadn't come by the time her man was plumb worn out.

But in this case, since they'd done right by one another in spite of the games they'd been playing, or mayhaps because of 'em, Judith Morrison was content to fall asleep in the arms of the killer she thought she'd recruited to her cause and, since he doubted she'd want to murder any man she'd hired to commit murders for her, Longarm felt safe enough to doze some, waking up to check her breathing every time they paused to drop off or take on mailbags every few miles as the night wore on.

They rolled south, east of the Front Range, at a fair clip until they swung west around the Sangre de Cristo fault block south of Las Vegas to forge on through rougher country a ways and hence south along the upper reaches of the south-flowing Rio Grande.

Had not it been so dark out, they'd have seen most of the pinpoints of lamplight they passed came from modest Mex milpas or bigger ranchero operations, a good many of them raising more mutton, pigs and chickens than beef. For a secret of the original vaquero was that, left to their druthers, most Spanish-speaking folk preferred pork, chicken or mutton, in that order, to beef. Mexicans had started out raising rawboned longhorn stock for tallow and hides. It had been the beef-eating Anglos who'd first considered serving longhorns for supper. Down Mexico way, where they still held bullfights every Sunday, the beef of the dead bull was served up to the poor folk in the neighborhood as charity. The Mexicans who'd paid to watch the elaborate knifing of a mighty dumb animal went home to dine on ham and sweet potatoes or chicken basted with chocolate and, like the Indians they'd taught the crafts to, Mexican women spun wool all day on the fly, walking about with spindles adangle at their sides to where they hardly noticed what they were up to. Mexican women sat different when they wove the threads they spun into sashes or scarves more often than blankets. But the designs were much the same, with the wool dyed the same way from the same gathered herbs. So whilst Mexicans and Indians fought as often as Indians and Anglos, if not more so, for religious reasons, Mexicans never fought anybody over sheep. Longarm knew the trouble, if trouble came, would start a day's drive or more west of the Rio Grande bottomlands. Giving him time to study on how in blue blazes they'd ever drive a thousand head of sheep through cowhands who'd learned their trade in West Texas.

That porter Judith had left a wake-up call with must have forgotten or fallen asleep his ownself. For she'd have slept right through had not the hired gun she thought she'd recruited woke her up with a kiss and then some in time for them to finish dressing as they were rolling into Albuquerque around four in the morning.

Longarm had slipped out of her compartment before the Rocking M hands who'd come to help her and her baggage off the train showed up to do this. So Longarm didn't get to watch. He dropped off a couple of platforms down and went to the baggage room in the D&RG depot to gather up his McClellan and lug it across to the Mountain View Hotel by the dawn's early light.

He'd told Judith he'd be staying there under an assumed name. She'd seen why he might not want to sign in as Latigo Shaw. Signing in as a well-known federal lawman

25

might have been dumber. So he signed as Buck Crawford and it would serve that Reporter Crawford of the *Denver Post* right if he read about himself in a rival paper.

Longarm's main reason for borrowing that particular name, however, was the need to keep track of such fibs and, aside from his little joke on Reporter Crawford, Longarm had always hoped he might be related to that Doctor Crawford Long who'd invented merciful ether, just in time for that painful showdown betwixt the states.

He asked at the desk if they'd wake him around eight A.M. He'd caught a few winks on the train and they said that famous Thomas Edison out of New Jersey got by on four hours sleep a day. Longarm figured if a man could invent phonographs, electric lights and such on four hours sleep he ought to be able to study some on sheepherding. He already knew how you herded cows.

Once in bed upstairs he warned himself not to study on shit until he had a handle on what was going on down this way. He'd learned in his boyhood, studying on how he was going to ask the blue-eyed gal to the hoedown, that no matter how you imagined what she'd say, she'd always say something different and you'd have to gather the eggs from where the hens had laid 'em. He'd never laid eyes on this BIA agent, Ed Dodsworth. He'd worry about what he ought to say to him after he'd heard what Dodsworth had to say.

As always, when he was in a strange bed or when he knew he had to rise and shine for early chores, Longarm was wide awake and washing up at the corner stand when the bellhop knocked on his door to say it was time to get up.

He changed his shirt but elected to stay with his dress-regulation duds until he saw what he might be up against. Neither Dodsworth nor anyone else had any call to ask at the desk for a guest named Crawford. So Longarm asked for Dodsworth and they told him the cuss was in the dining room, mad as a wet hen about something.

Hoping it wasn't him, Longarm ambled through the

archway where, sure enough, he found a heavyset gent in an undertaker's suit seated behind a stack of waffles he was only glaring down at, as if they'd just made a rude remark about his mother.

Longarm went over and remained on his feet as he asked if he had the honor of addressing a fellow government agent he was supposed to work with. Dodsworth was man enough to half rise and shake before he growled, "Have a seat and have some breakfast, Deputy Long. The goddamned son-of-a-bitching courthouse doesn't open until nine."

Longarm swung a chair from another table around and beckoned to a Mexican waiter as he mildly asked who they were taking to court.

Dodsworth replied, "His name is Chavez, Emilio Chavez. We contracted with him to assemble that Navaho herd for us from stockmen all around. They taught us in school that Queen Isabella drove all the Jews out of Spain. They taught us wrong. That Chavez jewed us good."

The waiter came over and Longarm ordered *huevos rancheros con café negro* before he asked if the sheep they'd contracted for were sick or lame or goats.

Dodsworth asked, "Do you speak Spanish?"

When Longarm modestly allowed he had enough Border Mex to get laid, the portly BIA agent said, "I'll want you with me at the courthouse. And I'd better show you what the problem is. Every damned New Mexican I've tried to talk to seems to think it's funny!"

Longarm pointed out he'd already ordered. Dodsworth said to go ahead and break his fast, but to be quick about it. So Longarm put away half the eggs and all the coffee and they were off and almost running.

As he led the way along the rail siding, Dodsworth complained the unpatriotic railroad was billing them for the use of the stockyard pens ahead. Longarm had served under officers who thought farmers who wanted to be paid for the food and fodder of an army column were profiteers. He knew better than to argue.

They passed some trackside loading chutes and a water tower and came to what seemed city blocks of stock pens to see, hear and smell how a sea of merinos milled in adjoining enclosures, each with its own watering *abrevadero con pesabra* to keep the critters watered and fed.

Longarm tried not to laugh as he caught sight of all those silly-looking sheep. It wasn't easy. The Spanish merino was most often viewed as a rangy surefooted breed most suited to the sunny hillsides and rough range the Spanish-speaking folk seemed drawn to, on either side of the Atlantic. As in that case of their long-horned cattle, the tough thrifty sheep tailored for the needs of the politically powerful Spanish wool trade was only *eaten* as an afterthought. The merino had roamed the hills of old Spain in ruinous numbers to provide the best wool to be had for the old world markets. There was a time when exporting merino breeding stock had been against the law in old Spain. Merino wool was still considered top-of-the-line in textile circles.

So, naturally, the enterprising contractor, Chavez, had delivered six thousand head fresh *shorn* and, whilst it probably made the sheep feel a mite friskier with summer coming on, a rangy merino sheep wearing what sure looked like flannel underwear was a pathetic sight to see.

Dodsworth almost shouted, "Don't laugh! I have it on good authority that Chavez sheared more than a thousand dollars worth of prime wool before he delivered the stock we'd contracted for!"

"Did you specify the stock was supposed to be delivered with or without said wool?" asked Longarm, wearily.

Dodsworth said, "Of course not. How were we to know the sneaky greasers would shear every fucking sheep in the dark of night? I want you with me when the courthouse on the plaza opens at nine. We'll show the greasers who they're dealing with. Goddamn their eyes!"

Longarm said, "Let's find a shady spot to set down and have a drink as I explain just what *you're* dealing with, out here, pard."

Chapter 4

For whatever reason the Anglo-speaking parts of Albuquerque, southeast of the old town closer to the river, had been laid out with streets called after numbers and avenues named for minerals, with the railroad station at First and Silver. So they moseyed up to Second and Gold where, sure enough, a sidewalk cantina offered set-down refreshments at sky-blue tables under a ramada of split cedar *tablillas*. Longarm ordered *cervezas*, sensing Dodsworth might not approve of tequila and knowing pulque was an acquired taste.

As they waited Longarm said, gently as he knew how, "You don't show *greasers* much in New Mexico Territory, pard. Mistaking New Mexico for, say, Texas has led to needless troubles for all concerned. When we took the Southwest from Old Mexico back in '48 lots of folk from the Old South headed west under the impression the Indians, Mexicans and colored folk were all darkies who knew their place and an Anglo-Saxon had a divine right to push them around."

The waiter brought their drinks. Longarm took a sip of suds before he went on. "That notion works where our kind has the numbers and political pull. Here in New Mexico we've neither. They called it *Nuevo Méjico* long before we

29

got here because Spanish-speaking pioneers forged up the Rio Grande in considerable numbers before those pilgrims landed on Plymouth Rock. They found the most civilized Indians north of Old Mexico already growing beans, corn, squash and tobacco around farming villages called *pueblos* in Spanish. They found out the hard way the Pueblo tribes were not sissies and, after some knock-down-drag-outs the Indians won, the New Mexicans learned to get along, convert and marry up with some, long as they respected the rights of others."

"Have you forgotten I work for the Bureau of Indian Affairs?" sniffed the older and stuffier Anglo, adding, "Say, isn't this *beer* you ordered?"

Longarm said, "They call it *cerveza*. Saves time out here when you ask for things their way. The fact that the combined races populated the hell out of *Nuevo Méjico* is only the half of it. There were plenty of mestizo or mixed-race Spanish-speaking papists out California way when our kind came horning in. Some few old Califorio clans adopted to our ways and still own some of their lands out yonder. But, as in Texas, they lost control of the courts and legislation. Some say, and it may be true, the Spanish way of life don't prepare a man for the rough-and-tumble world of Democracy. But here in New Mexico they got an unexpected break."

He sipped more suds and continued, "Professor Darwin might have called it natural selection, like a deer in rough times evolving into one of them giraffes to reach higher greenery. Nobody could have planned it, or guess how it might turn out, but about the time the Mexican War was set to start, they had this potato famine in Ireland. So a whole mess of Irish Catholics wound up on our side of the pond, where they weren't received too friendly by the mostly Protestant folk back East."

Dodsworth said, "That was over thirty years ago and those riots are a thing of the past."

Longarm smiled thinly and said, "I've pointed that out

to Irish beating up Chinee, more recent. Picking on folk who ain't like you seems to come natural to our species. The point is that back East there were signs in black and white that read NO IRISH NEED APPLY. But then, as now, the army was willing to take any recruit willing to get shot at for less than you'd have to pay a cowhand. So a heap of Irish Catholics joined up and not all of them were killed in the Mexican, Civil or Indian Wars. Heaps of 'em wound up out this way, where they discovered the Mexican señoritas were more than willing to court with fellow papists and, as a matter of fact, tended to look up to them."

Dodsworth sniffed and said, "Well, of course a greaser would look up to a *white* man, even a bead-mumbling Black Irishman."

Longarm said, "Bite your tongue. When Lucien Bonaparte Maxwell out of Illinois, where he hadn't been much, wed the Señorita Luz Beaubien, the Franco-Hispanic heiress of a Spanish land grant, it gave him the leg up to wind up owning more land, fee simple, than any other man in these United States."

He let that sink in before he added, "Along with fathering half a dozen New Mexico *greasers*, he founded the First National Bank of Santa Fe, helped finance the Texas Pacific Railroad and died in retirement a few years ago after buying a whole army fort off the war department to house his family and private army of servants. The railroad venture was ill-advised. His son, Pedro, or Pete Maxwell, is still one of the biggest rancheros in New Mexico. Do you need more?"

Dodsworth swallowed some suds with an expresson of distaste to say, "So some white Roman Catholics have found it easier to get rich out this way. What has that to do with the way Emilo Chavez cheated us?"

Longarm replied, simply, "It means we're shit out of luck before any judge we can take him before in New Mexico Territory. Folk from other parts call the setup the Santa Fe Ring and imagine secret meetings and such. It ain't that complexicated. Folk of all sorts look out for their own. Nobody has to hold a secret meeting in Texas when a Mexican gets arrested as a horse thief. It just stands to reason to your average Texas judge that a greaser brought before him by a Texican of good character has to be guilty."

"But Chavez sheared those sheep after we'd bought and paid for them!" the BIA agent protested.

Longarm smiled thinly and said, "I doubt old Emilio's likely Irish lawyer would phrase things that way. Take my advice and let it go. The wool will grow back and you're only going to tie things up in court for a month of Sundays if you push it."

"It's not just. You know I'd win before any impartial judge," Dodsworth protested.

Longarm shrugged and suggested, "Show me an impartial judge, and I'll show you a man who's never cast an admiring glance at pretty girl, or boy, as the case may be. Anglos who knew better tried to warn Uncle John Chisum and his young pals what would happen if they went up against the powers that was, in New Mexico. Uncle John and his pard, young Johnny Tunstall, still went on and hired a lawyer, Alexander McSween, and he was a Protestant from other parts as well."

Dodsworth asked, "Are we talking about that Lincoln County War? I read how members of the county political machine rode roughshod over newcomers who were only trying to break a trade monopoly."

Longarm drained his mug and signaled the waiter for two more before he said, "That's one way of looking at it. Try her another. What do you reckon might happen if an old windbag and two college boys swaggered into an Irish saloon, wearing orange shirts, to announce they were taking the joint over?"

Dodsworth laughed despite himself and asked, "Is that how they saw it, out this way?"

Longarm said, "Some did. Just after the war an army major of the Irish Catholic persuasion, Larry Murphy, took his discharge at Fort Stanton, down by the Mescalero Reserve, and set up a trading post with a Dutch sidekick, who died and ain't important to the story. Murphy started as a sutler, trading with the colored troops of the Ninth Cav before he moved into the nearby mushroom town of Lincoln Plaza to sort of grow with it. He had a younger associate, a rival merchant, matter-of-fact, named Jim Dolan, another Union vet. Dolan had an Irish pal named Ryan in the cattle business. Murphy acted as their agent, selling beef to the fort and the Indian agency. As the wide spot in the trail grew into a county seat they got this former first sergeant, Bill Brady, elected sheriff. Note nobody had done anything unlawful as they cut themselves a piece of the pie."

"I'd say they had a cozy deal," Dodsworth decided.

Longarm shrugged and said, "Professor Darwin calls it natural selection and that's the way small towns work the wide world over. Then a Johnny Reb of another faith driv a herd he'd never paid for up the Goodnight Trail from other parts, out to horn in on them profitable government beef sales. He formed a partnership with an adventuresome young Englishman from other parts and a Scotch Presbyterian out of Canada to commence a price and range war as proved disasterous to all concerned."

Dodsworth nodded and asked, "Didn't the corrupt Sheriff Brady have his deputies murder young Tunstall?"

Longarm replied, "Depends on which papers you read. They had a warrant sworn out lawsome. After they gunned Tunstall, McSween had his own justice of the peace swear a dozen young gunslicks as his own lawmen, badges and all, so Sheriff Brady was assassinated or shot resisiting arrest on April Fools' day."

He sipped some suds and added, "It was all over by midsummer, with all the important players dead or wishing they'd never commenced such a deadly game for so little profit. So why don't you forget trying to get anywhere in court against the current and let me see if I can manage the way things get done out here? I forgot to tell you those

Texas cattle folk have sent away for outside help, with five hundred dollars posted on your hide."

As expected, that seemed to get Dodsworth's undivided attention. So Longarm got to bring him up-to-date on his falling in with Judith Morrison, leaving out the dirty parts, of course.

When he got to where he'd parted company with Judith Morrison, with her still in the dark about his true identity, Dodsworth said, "She and her bunch must be insane. We're the federal government! They can't hope to stop us!"

Longarm nodded and said, "From what she said about that other gal on the same train, some of them don't. Maybe most of them don't. But one hothead up on a rimrock with a rifle can sure put a dent in our efforts and I was just about to remark on us being the federal government. Before I go into a plot worthy of Mr. Machiavelli, might I suggest a safer way?"

Dodsworth nodded and Longarm said, "I'd need a BIA survey map to be certain, but it seems to me from earlier trips that you all have a shit-house full of agencies out this way. Where in the way larger Navaho reseve are we supposed to deliver all them sheep?"

When Dodsworth said their Navaho agent and the tribal council would take possession at the Standing Rock trading post Longarm brightened and said, "There you go. That ain't as far as I feared and, like I said, you all have other wards of the government out this way. Say we just drove the herd south a ways, to ford the river at, say, Isleta, we'd be on BIA reservations west across the Rio Puerco and then if we swung north into your Luna reserve . . ."

"It's a day's drive south to the crossing you suggest!" Dodsworth cut in, adding, "We're already behind schedule and you want to drive the herd around Robin Hood's barn?"

Longarm soothed, "More like an extra week on a safer trail. We could zigzag almost due west across scattered Indian agency holdings, drive north almost due south of

Standing Rock and cross no more than twenty-five miles of white-held cattle country. Better yet, stockmen that far west ain't likely in with Judith Morrison's hotheads."

"What was the Machiavellian plot you had in mind?" asked Dodsworth. Longarm had been afaid he might.

He said, "Playing for time. Last night, I never told Judith Morrison I knew beans about you and the herd you only wanted to take *across* her range. If I was to contact her again, saying I'd been spying on you, and laughing fit to bust at her needless fears, she and her faction might see fit to live and let live. I'd naturally elaborate on what you said about it being a BIA herd under the protection of the federal government and I suspect the most sheep-hating Texan born of mortal woman would rather let a sheep pass by in peace than risk his ass and all he owns at the hands of a pissed-off Uncle Sam!"

Dodsworth said, "I like that plan better than attempting to drive six thousand head miles out of the way, short-handed, with the Navaho expecting us already!"

Longarm resisted the temptation to ask what the Navaho were supposed to do about it if they had to wait a spell for six thousand free sheep. It seemed more polite to ask how come they were already running so late.

Dodsworth said, "I don't have half the crew it will take to move six thousand head of sheep from here to Standing Rock, even with no opposition. We were planning on hiring local help before we found someone had put the word out against us. The professional sheepherders they keep sending me quit about as fast as they get here. I had some Basques, recruited from the Great Basin, tell me I didn't know my ass from my elbow and when I told them it just wasn't possible to hire an all-Basque crew they said it was that or nothing. They refused to work with Mexicans and laughed when I said we'd sent for some Anglo shepherds from back East."

Longarm nodded and said, "They say the Basques are the best in the business. But the Basques are mighty clannish and set in their ways. Have any of them other breeds of sheepherders showed up?"

Dodsworth sighed and said, "They have, speaking of set in their ways. It seems when you ask two sheepherders how to herd sheep you get thrcc strong opinions. Just yesterday this kilted wonder from the Highlands said it was no use because my sheep didn't understand the commands of his dogs."

Longarm chuckled and said, "Merinos likely don't speak Gaelic. I ain't certain, I wasn't taking notes the last time I rode through Navaho sheep country, but it did seem to me the Navaho keep small family flocks, each tended casual by the children within an easy walk for their spread-out hogans and held together by bells. I think they train one old sheep with a bell strung around its neck to follow the kid like a pup and the other sheep follow the . . . bellwether, they call it in English. Ain't certain how the local Mexicans may have trained all them sheep over yonder, but they do it with dogs. They can't be trained Scotch Highland style and Mexican dogs would act Mexican around Mexican sheep. I've watched sheepherders work summer flocks, up Colorado way. They whistle at their dogs. The dogs run this way and that to cut off strays by crouching low and just staring at them thoughful. They never bark and I've yet to see one nip. If the truth be known, sheep seem sort of stupid and I suspect the dogs train 'em from spring lambs to be obedient grazers."

Dodsworth sighed and said, "Great. I can't wait to see all those fool Mexican merinos learning to take orders from English-speaking dogs. In the meantime, I'll introduce you to my BIA staff and the crew we've gathered."

"I wish you wouldn't," Longarm said, adding, "I'm too young to die and Mr. Machiavelli would never approve if you expect me to get us through eighty miles of disputed range the risky way!"

36

Chapter 5

Some sardonic but wise old Frenchman had written it was
never a good notion to make love or have more than two
drinks before noon because you never knew who you might
run into at lunch time. So Longarm nursed his cerveza as
he tersely explained, "They got somebody spying on you,
other than the Latigo Shaw they just hired, and he'd be too
slick by half to just sashay up and ask for a job. He'd scout
you some, first. So that's what I aim to do. I aim to let it be
known around the stockyards I'm in the market for a job
guarding stock. That's how my hunting license reads. The
real Latigo Shaw would never ride over to the Rocking M
like a moon calf come a courting. He'd wait for Miss Judy
to contact him and ask how he was coming along. If she's
sincerely dangerous she'll give me time to work my way
into your confidence. She'll likely have some Mexicans
working for her and her bunch keeping an eye on me. Either way, I'll feel a heap safer selling her my bill of goods
here in town. With any luck we can convince her there's no
need for anybody to get hurt and if she tells me we have
her grudging permit, I can ride with you all as planned
whilst they laugh about it up on the rimrocks. Once we get
through the cattle crowd and make it to Standing Rock
without getting raided by the others, we can let the happy

37

Navaho worry about parceling out the herd, two or three dozen to a family, see?"

Dodsworth said, "Hold on. What was that about *others*? Are you saying the range hogs who've moved in to former Navaho land may not be all we have to contend with?"

Longarm nodded soberly and said, "The local boys have already had a good laugh at your expense by shearing you out of all that wool. Who's to say nobody would be tempted by all that prime breeding stock, seeing they already have you down as a gringo *pendejo* if not a *pobrecito*?"

"You've made my day," muttered Dodsworth wearily.

Then he said, "All right. How do you want to work it out with me?"

Longarm said, "Give me the day to establish some character and see if I can seperate some bad apples from the local barrel. Seeing we're staying at the same hotel across from the railroad I'll just meet up with you some more and you can tell your own crew you've hired me, under the name of Crawford, as a shotgun rider. I'll make myself to home as you all get better organized and with any luck, those cattle folk concerned about sheep crowding in on 'em ought to contact me well before we can be ready to move."

Longarm rose to his considerable height, leaving more than enough jingle to pay for their drinks on the sky-blue table and suggested, "Why don't you go on about your own beeswax whilst I scout some? I mean to circle back to the hotel another way and change into more suitable duds for down this way. Once I look more stockyard I'll set out to make some friends in low places. No telling who I might wind up plotting against you with if I'm taken for a *pícaro bueno* or one of the boys."

Dodsworth said he followed the drift and they each went their own way for the time being. Longarm gave the older man a head start by drifting northwest to the older part of town where, still wearing a gringo suit and tie, he had no trouble asking to go through their registered brands at the hall of records.

He fished out his notebook and a pencil stub to note the mailing addresses of the Rocking M and that Double W Judith had mentioned in connection with a more sensible neighbor opposed to range wars. When he saw how both spreads lay along the same Arroyo Chico, overlooked by the rimrocks of a Mesa Chivato, he muttered, "Shit God fucking damn!" For that looked like a swell route to drive a whole lot of livestock with high summer coming on.

Six thousand sheep would need a lot of water and did you move 'em up the far side of the tanglewood you usually found along running water in semiarid country, marksmen on the mesa to the southwest would have a time picking off man or beast on the move.

But, as was only natural and as other registered brands assured him, a whole shithouse full of spanking new cattle barons had claimed their usual quarter section home spreads along that steady supply of water and firewood. The federal Homestead Act was a joke in the marginal range of natural cattle country. You couldn't grow enough truck or even barley on 160 acres to pay. But once you had your home spread in place, with mayhaps a kitchen garden, some hogs to slop and a chicken or more to supply eggs for breakfast, you got to graze your livestock on the unclaimed open range all around and *that*, Virginia, was why there really were such things as range wars. The outfits who got there first, to claim their own mere fractions of all the range there was, didn't want anybody else horning in to claim the nigh deserted land they were grazing as if they owned it.

As he studied the numbers of new brands betwixt Albuquerque and the dryer land still held by the Navaho nation off to the northwest, Longarm decided Judith Morrison and her Texas crowd were already pushing their luck. That many cattle outfits on that amount of marginal range added up to overgrazing at the best of times and worried minds when the thunder birds got to sulking. Such rain as they got in that stretch of the high and dry Colorado Plateau came mostly in the form of vagrant summer cloud bursts moving up out of the southeast *against* the prevailing west winds, wrung mighty dry by the higher mountains out California way.

On the map it read the Continental Divide ran down out of Colorado through west New Mexico. But the Rocky Mountains were more tricky in the real world than across any paper map and, as in the case of the more famous South Pass up Wyoming way, you hardly noticed how high you were as you moved from the drainage of the Rio Grande to that of the eastern canyon lands of the mightier Colorado.

There were higher stetches, wooded with cedar, juniper and pinyon pine along that dotted line on the map. But the range between the Rio Grande and the Navaho land, range now claimed by Judith Morrison and her Texas pals, was mostly chaparral with short grass and seasonal forbs between, Lord willing and the cows didn't graze it faster than it could grow.

He knew cattlemen said range had been *sheeped off* when it had been grazed clean to the roots, whether there were any sheep within miles or not. Sheep outfits could be just as pigheaded when their own overgrazing stock ruined range innocent of any cows. It went againt human nature to admit mistakes. It was bad luck, or somebody else's fault, when you bet the rent money on a roll of the dice and lost.

Having a better grasp of the lay of the disputed land, and still liking his alternate route through Indian lands to the south way better, Longarm went back to his hotel to get rid of his fool tie and gringo duds, and change into faded but clean and way thinner denim. He felt cooler in the shade of his hotel room and if the six-gun on his hip rode more exposed, Albuquerque wasn't one of those sissy towns like

Dodge where they asked a man who'd never made a move
to draw what he was wearing that there gun for.

The railroad had just recently brought more of the outside world in to a tight-knit town where nobody asked
questions of any man they had any reason to respect.
Founded in the early 1700s and named after a Spanish
duke and viceroy of New Spain, Albuquerque had spent
the better part of two centuries as a dusty trail town betwixt
Old Mexico and the action up around Santa Fe. It was just
getting used to being an American town. The older parts
around the plaza and adobe church of San Felipe de Neri
still looked, smelled and sounded as if you were in Old
Mexico. And though newcomers moving in kept talking
about incorporating a more Anglo municipal government,
it hadn't happened yet and that seemed the way a heap of
residents, Spanish- or English-speaking, seemed to want
things.

Albuquerque was still governed Mexican-style, meaning the less formal ways they'd taken up after getting shed
of their royal Spanish notions.

They had an *alcalde* and council of respected elders,
meaning heads of important local families who, being *pa-
trones* as well as council members, got to back their polite
suggestions with devoted armed and dangerous riders.
They said that in his day old Lucien Maxwell had never
worn a gun and felt no call to after meeting an Apache war
party unarmed and mildly pointing out that he had more
riders on his payroll that the U.S. Army had west of the
Mississippi.

It wasn't a better way or a worse way to keep the peace,
in Longarm's view. It was just *different*, and he felt that
when in Rome it was best not to bang your head against
adobe walls.

Dressed more cow, he moseyed back over to the stockyards, lighting a cheroot to smoke as he leaned his elbows
on a rail to marvel at all those nigh naked sheep. They

41

didn't seem embarrassed. Like himself, they likely felt cooler with all that greasy wool off. It was the natural waxy oils evolved to shed rain from living sheep that some folk found so rancid. Goats smelled worse because they had musk glands to advertise they were in the mood for fornication. Cow shit didn't smell so bad to Anglo folk who were used to it and nobody paid much mind to horse shit in a world running on horse and steam power.

This Chinee gal Longarm had enjoyed some pillow conversation with had assured him white folk smelled like rancid butter to her kind, albeit she'd forgiven him. It made more sense after she'd explained nobody in China et dairy products. It was smells you weren't used to that got you to suspecting something bad was in the air. The smell of canned sardines could empty a trading post of Navaho or Mescalero, whilst some white eyes found the smoky corn husk aroma of Navaho hogans unsettling.

"Ain't that a comical spectacle?" asked a voice to Longarm's right and, when he glanced that way, he saw it came from a jockey-sized sandy-haired squirt with features Irish as Paddy's pig. His accent sounded raised in the American West, however, as he confided, "Some new sheep outfit bought all them merinos without mention of their wool and so the Mexicans made better than an extra thousand on the deal by delivering 'em as you see."

"I was wondering if they were sheep," Longarm replied with a dry smile, adding, "Heard they'd been trying to sign on drovers. Wish I knew more about sheep than cows. I got handed the shovel up Cimarron way and can't seem to land a job in these parts."

The little Irishman said, "No shit? None of my beeswax, of course, but what excuse might they have given when they fired you, Mister . . . ?"

"Crawford. Call me Buck. I never got laid off for stealing or even shirking honest chores. The ramrod asked me to muck out the stables after he saw me dancing with a gal he fancied, in town, on my own time."

"I had a boss like that one time. Shot the son of a bitch a year later, so's nobody would suspect me. I'd be Gluepants Gafferty. A bronco buster by trade. I rode for a sheep outfit out Nevada way one time. You wouldn't like it. I only worked a few weeks on a market drive. No white man can herd sheep without going soft in the head."

"I didn't know there was that much difference," Longarm cautiously confessed.

Gluepants shrugged and said, "There ain't, when it comes to *driving*. A bunch of old boys on horseback drive most any stock, from cows to hogs to turkeys much the same. It's sort of like sweeping dust out the door with brooms. You just ride to cut off any critter who ain't going the way you want 'em all to go, waving your throw ropes and cussing their mothers 'til they sense they're safer moving the way the rest of the herd, flock, gaggle or whatever seems to be going."

He reached for a smoke of his own as he pontificated. "A drive is a drive, aimed at moving stock from where it's at to where you want it. I ain't certain, but I think this sheep outfit I rode for that time put their stock out on higher range in late spring to graze away as they growed a crop of wool against the coming winter, then druv 'em back down to their home spread in late fall to shear, sell or shelter. I wasn't there when they rutted with their rams. They mostly lambed in early spring, fenced in where the coyotes attracted to the smell couldn't get at 'em. The permanent hands saw to docking the tails and cutting off the nuts of the he-lambs. They were over their bawling and ready to go by the time us hired-on drovers druv 'em back up to their summer range."

Longarm asked how sheep were grazed along the way.

Gluepants said, "Same as cows. Ain't nothing tricky about driving any critter that eats what's growing there, do you have enough *riders*. You try to end the day's drive near water on good grazing ground. Then all you have to do is mount a night rider or more to circle the herd and keep it

43

bunched. Most natural herding stock tends to keep bunched after dark on its own. The night rider just has to keep moving a ways out to remind any independent thinker there's bigger critter moving out yonder in the dark. The time I tell of, we found sheep easier to hold to a steady pace on the trail after the first breaking-in morning. Sheep don't run fast as cows. So they're way easier to head off."

Longarm asked how many miles you could drive sheep in a day.

Gluepants thought and decided, "Eight or ten miles. I'd say. They get harder to drive towards the end of the day unless you tolerate 'em some grazing along the way at a slow walk. But there ain't no big deal about it with plenty of riders on faster riding stock."

They were joined by another hand with nothing better to look at. When he howdied Gluepants and asked what he was missing, the little Irishman soberly replied, "We was trying to decide if that fat ass ewe with the waggly tail wants us to screw her or not. This here's Buck Crawford, Dallas. I've been trying to turn him into a sheepherder because his cock's too small for cows."

Dallas grinned at Longarm and said, "Old Gluepants has never got over the loss of his true love, served as lamb chops even if she *was* getting too old to dance the hoolihan. Why don't we continue this conversation over at the La Posada Pilar, where they say the barkeep takes it in the ass if you can't make a deal his wife?"

So the three of them ambled west with the morning sun now beating down on the backs of their shoulders and as they entered the taproom of a trackside inn and drinking establishment, they found the place starting to crowd up with other thirsty locals trying to avoid the noonday sun.

The regulars Longarm had come in with seemed to feel no introductions were needed as the others accepted him as somebody who hung out with good old boys they knew. As they bellied up to the bar, Gluepants said to nobody in particular, "We were just talking about those bare-ass sheep over by the tracks."

An older and way taller rider down the bar said, "Heard they'd been put together for a drive to McKinley County by some outsider called Doodlebug."

Another there snorted, "Dodsworth. Says he works for the BIA and aims to give all them sheep, free, to Mister Lo, the poor Indian, the lying son of a bitch. Offering a dollar a day and found to any rider foolish enough to drive sheep into cattle country."

More than one rider assembled whistled thoughtfully. The one who seemed to know so much said, "Don't even think about it. Word's already out how them Texican rancheros up yonder have sent away for help, and Dodsworth ain't in with any of the local sheep men. If he *was*, he'd still be setting out to start a war that ought to make that one down in Lincoln County look like a Sunday School picnic!"

Chapter 6

Few of the Anglo railroad workers, stockyard hands and such who worked in the newer parts of Albuquerque east of Fifteenth Street had truck with the old town's Spanish customs of *La Siesta*. Longarm knew better and he was still inclined to feel a tad guilty about doping off in the shank of the day from say noon to three or four. But he knew nothing or nobody he wanted to scout up in the old town would be up and about until *La Siesta* was over, and besides, he'd had a rough night.

His first thought was to head back to the Mountain View before it got hotter. That was the reason Spanish-speaking folk had adopted the custom from North African Moor in the first place. The dry dazzling sunlight in the sort of country Spanish-speaking folk gravitated to could heat stroke mad dogs and English speakers who ran around outside at high noon. Those who'd grown up in such climes found it more sensible to hole up indoors, bare ass in bed, to toss and turn sweaty if the humidity was high, or enjoy a swell nap, with or without company, until it was safe to go outside some more. The part so many disapproving yanquis missed, when they went on about lazy Mexicans, was how Mex business establishments from banks to whorehouses stayed open way later at night than back East where the Protestant work ethic prevailed. Spanish-speaking visitors to towns such as Boston or New York City reported with considerable disgust how you couldn't cash a check or shop for shoes after sundown because all the lazy *gringos chingados* had closed for the night.

Feeling a sincere need for a bare-ass flop, and aiming to parlay his acceptance as someone who belonged in Albuquerque, Longarm took the fat barkeep cum *posadero* aside to ask if he might wrangle a room to siesta in upstairs. The older Mex seemed to find his request sensible and so he turned "Buck Crawford" over to a short *mestiza* getting around barefoot in her gathered calf-length skirts and low-cut cotton blouse. She wore her ebony hair in bangs, cut collarbone length, Pueblo style, and said she was called Pilar.

When Longarm asked if she was the Pilar who owned the place she said that had been her late grandmother. Her *papacito* owned the place, now. That was her *tío* or uncle behind the bar. She seemed to be holding something back. Longarm felt as if they'd met before as well. He knew better than to ask a moderately pretty gal if he hadn't seen her someplace before.

Pilar led him to a steep stairway in the back. He admired the view as he followed her up. She wasn't wearing anything under her billowing skirts. He told himself to behave. Making a play for a Spanish-speaking gal under her father's roof could get a man killed even if they weren't better than half Indian.

Pilar led him to a corner room with cross ventilation provided by narrow windows set at right angles in the thick adobe walls, each one shaded by Morosco gridwork of brick-red terra-cotta. The bedstead sat in the middle of the modest-sized room, with each leg set in a shallow brass bowl of soapy water. Any harvester ants or scorpions out to disturb the rest of any guest of La Posada Pilar had their work cut out for them and Longarm said so.

As he reached in his jeans for a tip little Pilar commenced to cry.

Longarm gravely told her, "I mean you no disrespect, Señorita Pilar. I know you ain't in *servicidad* to your own proud family. It's a custom of my people to offer *dar una propina* when somebody does something for us."

She sighed and sobbed, "I am not so sad *a causa por eso*. I weep when I remember you said I was *muy linda* and now you no longer remember me, *El Brazo Largo!*"

Longarm muttered, "Dirty birds and teeny turds!" as he stepped around her to shut the hall door. He knew better than to say he didn't know what she was talking about. He said, "I was hoping you might not remember me, *querida*. I'm here on a mission *muy en secreto*. Can I count on your *fidelidad* to *la causa*?"

She stared up goggled-eyed to swear he could fuck her with hot pokers and she'd never betray him or *la causa de Méjico libre!*

Having had a peek up under her skirts, he wished she'd chosen another way of putting that. He already felt guilty about the way he had to bullshit the sweet little thing.

In truth as a paid up deputy U.S. marshal it was no never-mind to Longarm how the good folk of Old Mexico governed their own country. Knowing more of its history than some of them out to govern it, Longarm took Mexican patriots with a pinch of salt. The current cocksucker in charge, *El Presidente* Porfirio Diaz, had commenced his own career under Juarez as a hard-fighting rebel against the dictatorship of the French puppet emperor, Maximilian. When Juarez died under an all-too-short spell of sensible government his General Diaz declared himself president in his place and things had gone to hell in a hack, to hear most Mexicans Longarm knew tell it. But when you got right down to it a heap of his own United States seemed run for their own fun and profit by blatant crooks who somehow got dead folk and fairies in the bottom of their garden to vote 'em in every time. So Longarm would have been content to live and let live the times he'd trailed a U.S. Federal Warrant south of the border. But *Los Rurales*, the Diaz dictatorship's answer to the Texas Rangers, had from the beginning set out to execute a pesky gringo they described on their own WANTED posters as *El Brazo Largo* or "the long arm," with results they might have forseen had they known who they were messing with.

Mex rebels such as the notorious *El Gato* and the mighty pretty *La Mariposa* had decided with as little invite to declare *El Brazo Largo* one of their own and tales were told down Mexico way, some of them true, of the hard times *El Brazo Largo* and his Mex rebel pals had given *Los Rurales chingados* or "fucking rangers."

Billy Vail had patched up a truce with the officious Mex law for a spell. But sore losers related to losers Longarm had shot it out with were forever sendings *buscadores* after him. So Billy Vail had ordered him to stop invading Mexico and Longarm tried to quit as sincerely as he often tried to quit smoking.

Like Mark Twain, Longarm didn't see what all the fuss was about when it came to quitting smoking. Like Mark Twain, he'd often quit smoking more than twice a month.

In the meantime, as *El Brazo Largo*, a deputy U.S. marshal only trying to do his job had more friends and foes amongst the Mex community of the southwest than he felt he needed. Working-class Mex-Americans who still sent money home were always pestering him to let them help him overthrow *El Presidente*. Easy money boys, or just border *buscadores* who didn't cotton to Anglos, were as often out to carry the head of *El Brazo Largo* back to Old Mexico for the dead or alive bounty posted on it on the sly.

He mentioned this right off to little Pilar, laying it on a tad but not too much when he confided, "I'm here under an assumed name. If word as to my true identity got out I could wind up shot in the back within the hour. I don't know how many *enemigos* are after me or what any of

50

them look like. My only hope is that they don't know I'm in town to investigate them, *comprende*?"

She moved closer and he noticed she had jasmine scent mixed with her clean womanly sweat as she assured him, "You can build houses on me and my people. We don't have to tell anyone else, downstairs, but unless my *Tío* Hector know for why I am spending so much time alone with you he will suspect we have dishonored the family and you know what sort of trouble that could get him into!"

Longarm did. That was another reason he got along better than some with Mexicans. He knew how many of them would just smile and shrug if you called 'em lazy thieving bastards, then charge head down with a serious weapon, against impossible odds, because somebody mentioned a female of his family that somebody hadn't been introduced to, formal.

You didn't want to act as if you thought a Mex was afraid of you, either. He had to prove he wasn't, even if it meant the both of you died together in a blaze of glory. Longarm had often wondered why old Diaz, being Mex himself, albeit he wore face powder to make his fool self look whiter, didn't understand how he pissed off all those Mexicans down home by acting like such a bully. They'd likely pay his fool taxes and work on his damn roads, free, if he had the sense to ask polite. On one occasion, in Laredo, Longarm had seen a *Rurale* swagger into a cantina three sheets to the wind, demand a drink, wink at a gal seated with a barefoot peon and catch a bullet right betwixt the eyes.

Nobody there had asked the barefoot peon for why he'd just murdered a government official and he'd known without being told it was time to run for the hills and take up banditry for a living.

Pilar murmured she'd be right back. He didn't try to talk her out of it. He knew that once you were spotted, you swore a very few to secrecy or you could count on it being all over town by sundown. But he paced nervously trying to come up with another way and wondering what could be

51

keeping Pilar until all of a sudden she was back, shutting and barring the door behind her as she chortled, "Is all settled. While *El Brazo Largo* is in Albuquerque I am to obey his every wish as if I had been given to him *en iglesia* by *El Obisbo*, no?"

Longarm started to say they didn't have to carry things that far.

Then he wondered why any natural man would want to say a dumb thing like that, seeing Pilar seemed to be taking off her clothes.

Knowing *La Siesta* offered them time to spare and not wanting to waste any of it arguing with a woman, Longarm hung his Stetson on one bedpost, his six-gun on another and sat down on the edge of the bed to start with his boots. But Pilar, having such a head start in just her loose skirts and pullover blouse, was already bare of ass and coming around to drop to her knees adoringly and help him shuck his boots.

Without her Hispanic costume she looked more Indian as the little light from outside revealed her smooth, tawny contours. She was built chunkier than your average white gal that pretty. But there was no flab to her stocky thighs as she hunkered on them holding a booted foot up close to her firm brown breasts to haul it off as if she'd done it before. He knew she likely had, but he felt mighty sure she'd never hauled *his* boots off for him in the past. So where was he supposed to remember her from? He knew he'd lost a lot of ground he'd gained if he confessed he just plain didn't remember where he'd seen those big doe eyes staring out under those Pueblo bangs at him like so.

They got the other boot off him and then as long as she was down there she commenced to haul his jeans off as he shucked his demim bolero and unbuttoned his hickory shirt.

Then she had his old organ grinder in hand to marvel at how she'd had no right to expect so much honor before she kissed it sweetly and rose to shove him back across the mattress and honor herself to the roots as she impaled her chunky self on his suddenly raging erection.

It felt too teasingly good to abide, so after she'd honored herself to where she commenced to slow down, Longarm rolled her on her back to honor her with an elbow hooked under each of her tawny knees, with his socks on the bare planks and the edge of the mattress hooked under her tailbone, until he fired his first salvo into her shuddering orgasm.

After that they got into a more sensible position atop the bedding to do it right until they just had to come up for air and after a long lingering kiss, at both ends, they wound up sharing a smoke, propped up friendly against the head of the bed.

As Longarm took the cheroot back betwixt his own teeth Pilar sighed and marveled, "Was even better than I dreamed and I have dreamed of it many times since that night on the balcony overlooking the Rio Brazos. I was so confused, with my desires so conflicted, as we cooled between dance sets with that night-blooming jasmine scenting the breezes off the water and both of us knowing I was the woman of Francisco."

A tumbler in the combination lock clicked. Longarm blew a thoughtful smoke ring and asked, "Are you and old Francisco still together?" as he recalled that safe house where he and *El Gato* had holed up with the fool *Rurales* beating the stickerbrush along the crossing for the both of them.

Pilar answered, simply, "He went down fighting when someone betrayed him at *La Fiesta Brava*. Friends got me across the Rio Bravo before *Los Rurales* came after me. I came home. My parents forgave me for running away with a man of more heart as well as more Indian blood. As you must have seen, downstairs, I prefer to work here in town where things seem more exiting than out on the Granja Amendez, where every day is much the same, day after day after day."

Longarm brightened and said, "Your folk run a farm as well as this good-sized posada in town?"

She shrugged a bare shoulder against him to reply, "Of course. We are not a family to be despised. My people have farmed a good many *campos*, here and there, north of the city, for a good many years. Neither of my parents were born landless *pobrecitos*. In addition to this posada my family operates other businesses in town. But my father has his younger brothers in charge of them. He has always said a man who does not look after his own land soon has no land for to look after, *comprende*?"

Longarm said, "Our agriculture professors warn about what they describe as absentee land management and advise against it. So your dad sounds as if he's read up on the subject. But you'd rather wait tables here in town?"

She reached down to fondle his flaccid manhood as she slyly asked him, "Would we have met again, after all this time, if I had been content for to tend my father's flocks like your, how do you call her, Little Bo Peep?"

Longarm asked, "Your dad has flocks of *sheep* out yonder as needs tending, Pilar?"

She snuggled closer, getting a better grip, as she replied in a not too enthusiastic tone, "Sheep, pigs, chickens, even *pavos chingados*. I think you would say *fucking turkeys*. Big *estupidos* who murder their children and commit suicide if you do not watch them every *momento*. For why do you ask, *El Brazo Largo*? You were not planning to start your own *granja* for to raise *pavos chingado*, were you?"

Longarm laughed and replied, "I'm more interested in how your own folk handle *sheep*. Some pals of mine seem stuck with a thousand head of Mex merino sheep and no Mex *pastores* to move them over a hundred of our miles as everybody can *agree* on. You reckon your dad would be willing to talk to me about the herding of sheep for fun and profit in these parts?"

Pilar thought and decided, "We would have to tell him who you were. As I said, we are not a family to be despised

54

and Jesus Amendez is famous for his sense of honor the length of El Río Bravo. If I can tell him I have been fucking *El Brazo Largo* and not just a handsome gringo, I shall take you home with me for a dinner, and dessert, you shall long remember, *querido mío!*"

Chapter 7

There was no discreet way for a local *mestiza* to bring a strange gringo home to dinner without the neighbors noticing. But by the time *La Siesta* was over they'd worked out some swell positions and the best way to work it.

Since her dad was a *comerciante grande* and since Spanish-speaking folk of quality, or assuming the airs of quality, seldom sat down to the dinner table earlier than nine P.M. she only had to give him the simple directions and he could ride out after dark.

In the meantime she'd have knocked off work for the day downstairs a tad early and gone out to her family farm, plainly alone, in the soft light of the gloaming. That would give her plenty of time to soften her old man up and swear him to secrecy. She hardly needed to tell Longarm there was no way in hell he was about to sleep with her under the roof of Don Jesus Amendez. He slyly suggested he could hardly wait until it was siesta time, *mañana*.

So they parted friendly for the time-being at four and Longarm went back to his hotel. At the desk they told him a lady had been by, earlier than noon, asking for him. Longarm told them to tell her, if she came by again, he'd be out some more until around midnight.

Then he went up to fetch his saddle and bridle before he asked for directions to the nearest horse trader. They advised him he didn't have far to tote his load, seeing he'd find one at First and Copper.

He was just as glad he didn't have to trudge farther, even though by then the late afternoon shade extended clean across the dusty street. It still *smelled* like the inside of a brick oven as the adobe walls all around still radiated some.

He found the horse trader they'd told him about to be an old Anglo who ran a livery service and saddle shop as well. He said they called him Pop. Longarm knew a horse trader they called Pop shared many of the same qualities you'd expect from a gambling man they called Doc. So when Pop said he had just the horse to go with that army saddle Longarm forked over a corral rail, Longarm allowed he'd as soon decide such matters for himself and asked to see the whole line.

Pop had his stable boy produce a dozen old nags in various states of disrepair when Longarm allowed he'd go no higher than twenty, adding he didn't need more than a steady trotter.

As the horses milled around the corral Pop opined he was likely in the market for one of his three retired cavalry mounts, adding, "Pony as can cut and rope's worth more than twenty at any age."

Longarm was too polite to tell an older man he was full of shit. There were in fact three taller bay mounts mixed in, all three looking dusty and dispirited to be associating with cow ponies. Longarm knew the Army Remount Service sold stock off at eight years, with some good years left in them, because by then it got tough to tell just how old a horse was by the telltale wear of its teeth.

As the adult teeth of a horse wore down, an inner ring of enamel called its *infundibulum*, a sort of tooth inside a tooth, got ever smaller, like a shrinking bull's-eye until, at around seven years, there was only a bitty bull's-eye and then, by the time a horse was eight, an ominous brown stain of softer tooth pulp joined the mere dot of inner enamel and Lord only knew what was fixing to happen next.

Horses didn't seem to worry about such matters. Longarm had ridden mounts with fair-sized pulp cavities and no infundibulum at all. But the remount officers wanted to know how old a mount was before they sent a soldier blue out on it. So they sold stock off at eight years old and a man could get a real bargain, if he *guessed* right.

An eight- or ten-year-old horse could still win races. A horse going on twenty wasn't going very far very fast.

Knowing the brain of a horse was geared more for memory than for new problems to solve, Longarm climbed up in the corral rails to surprise Pop and the milling stock by suddenly singing out in a hearty baritone voice, to the familiar cavalry tune about the girl they'd left behind them . . .

> "Oh, she jumped in bed and covered up her
> head, And swore I'd never find her!
> But I knew damned well she lied like hell,
> So I jumped right in behind her!"

As expected, three sets of ears and those ears alone perked up as they heard an old parade ground march. Longarm watched closely as they milled on by and sang:

> "I belong in the cavalry.
> And don't you think I oughtter?
> When I get paid I wanna get laid,
> And I show the gals no quarter!"

Then he told Pop he wanted a tighter look at that mare who'd pranced to the familiar tune.

Pop said her name was Dancer and she was worth twenty-five if she was worth a red cent. So Longarm was able to beat him down to fifteen.

As they were saddling her with Longarm's McClellan, Dodsworth from the BIA caught up with him. He said they'd told him at the hotel Longarm might be there and asked how come he'd just bought a horse, observing they had their own remuda in the hotel stable.

Longarm led Dancer up the street out of earshot before he told Dodsworth, "I don't work for you, yet. Don't look back, but there's a Mex kid who ought to wear a less-imposing sombrero and he followed me here from the hotel. So I reckon this is about the time I ought to be dickering with you for that job. Since you were just seen looking for me, I reckon you heard at the hotel I'd been asking around about all them sheep. One of the reasons I like to work alone is the way pals like you fuck up stories I might have told another way!"

Dodsworth smiled sheepishly and said, "All right, I just hired you as an armed guard, having noticed those tailored grips on that double-action .44–40 and I see your saddle gun's a repeating Winchester '73, too. Come back to the hotel with me and meet the others you'll be riding with."

Longarm shook his head and said, "Not hardly. Not yet. The less they know about me the less they can blab about me. I've been invited to dine with a local *comerciante* or 'merchant-rancher' out on the outskirts of town. His daughter says he raises all sorts of stock, including sheep, and with any luck he grubstakes full-time sheepherders in these parts. That's the way Mexicans are. They ain't as independent as our frontier settlers and that's how come they don't go broke or starve to death as often. Mex communities are all intermeshed in a complexicated manner, with the poor relations provided for at the bottom and most everybody owing somebody a tad richer until you get all the way up to the grandee who thinks he's God but never lets on if he has a lick of sense."

He broke stride to add, "*El Presidente* Diaz ain't got a lick of sense. I'm hoping the Don Jesus I'm dining with this evening will be easier to get along with."

"Why?" asked Dodsworth, simply.

Longarm replied, "Weren't you listening? I just told you the man knows the local *sheep* business. You just got skinned by a *comerciante* Amandez likely drinks with. I don't know toad squat about sheepherding, neither. Don't you think it's about time one of us did?"

Dodsworth sniffed, "That's why I've asked them to send us professional sheep men, Deputy Long."

Longarm said, "Call me Buck. Get used to that. I've already commenced to wonder about that one Scotch sheepherder you said you'd hired. I'll likely be able to say for certain by the time I get back. I mean to ask just how a sheep dog communicates with sheep. The few times I've watched, nobody said shit in any lingo. The sheepherder whistles shrill enough to be heard half a mile away and the dog just runs silent to cut off sheep its master is concerned about, no?"

Dodsworth conceded, "If you say so. MacTavish claims to have had lots of experience."

Longarm mounted up as he snorted, "Seldom see a man applying for any job saying he had no experience at all. First lie you learn, looking for your first job. We'll study on MacTavish later. Why don't we talk about it at breakfast time, come morning?"

Dodsworth called after him, "It's a deal, then, Buck!" as Longarm rode away. Dodsworth was learning. Longarm heeled Dancer into a lope north on First Street, heedless of the puzzled looks they were drawing as the two of them tore past the railroad station. He didn't look back to see if that Mex kid in the imposing sombrero was running after them on foot. He knew the curious young shit couldn't hope to keep them in sight, no matter who he was working for.

When they came to Gold Avenue Longarm reined Dancer east across the rail yards instead of west toward the usual action. The old army bay was as spirited as he'd hoped and by the time they'd cut between parked boxcars and loped a furlong into the new consruction mushrooming over that way he was pretty certain nobody was following them. He'd likely thrown them an unexpected curve by suddenly loping out of sight on horseback after traipsing around all day in his old army boots.

East of the tracks, since they'd used up numbers to the west of 'em, the new northsouth streets had names, such as John Street, with yet another Broadway lined with mostly vacant lots and FOR SALE signs. He rode on to where the streets seemed named after trees such as Elm, Locust, Oak, Mulberry and such to see colored folk staring thoughtfully at him from the dooryards of frame cabins. The cabins, like the railroad to his rear, looked recent. You usually saw a fairly prosperous colored quarter in any fair-sized railroad town. The railroads, like the army, offered as fair a day's pay for a hard day's work as anyone was likely to offer your average colored man. That song about working on the railroad was sung a lot less mournful than "Down in the Cornfield."

At that hour most of the colored menfolk would be working on the railroad, all the live long day. Their women were shucking peas or peeling spuds for suppertime whilst the kids played kick the can and such in the lengthening shadows. The point was that few Texas riders would be likely to have spies planted in the colored quarter and nobody he passed seemed all that interested in him.

So when he came to Spruce Street he followed it south at a lope until he was riding alone across open desert.

He rode on south to where he was following no road at all as Dancer picked her way through patches of low chaparral across unbroken desert pavement, the brittle crust of birdcage gravel pasted together by calcite salts where rain was a sometimes thing.

Dead certain, now, he'd thrown off anybody tailing him, Longarm rode into the sunset towards the river and the Camino Real running alongside as far north as Santa Fe.

It was still light enough to see a country mile. So he stopped at a roadside *cafetín* on the southwest outskirts of town to kill some time as he waited for darkness to fall.

He ordered pulque when they confessed they had no beer. Then he asked for hot tamales with a bowl of chili to kill two birds at once. Pulque was to tequila what sour mash was to bourbon. It was an acquired taste few Anglos acquired but it was wetter than nothing and eating something along with it would mop up some of the alcohol in the sneaky potion of fermented cactus juice. Longarm knew he'd be lucky to sit down to dine by nine, out to the Amendez spread, and he was used to eating a tad closer to six.

So he took his time, flirting some with the fat gal behind the counter until they could barely see one another. When she lit a candle stuck on a wine bottle he ordered a slice of tuna pie, washed down with tolerable black coffee, and made certain Dancer had been watered and foddered out back before he mounted up to ride on. He rode through town at a walk to time it about right. Pilar had told him to look for pueblo ruins betwixt the stage route to Gallup and Candeleria Road. So he did and they surely rose bleak and spooky by moonlight. So he headed east some more until he saw paper lanterns glowing every color along the veranda of a rambling *casa grande* and when he rode into it to ask if it was by any chance the Amendez place he was greeted like a long-lost favorite uncle. A couple of young stable hands wrestled for the reins of old Dancer and Pilar came out in the yard, wearing shoes and gussied up in white Spanish lace, to take possession of her own caballero, thank you very much!

As she led him into the house Pilar murmured, *"Mi padre* knows all. I most naturally got him to swear nobody else will know who you are or for what you are here. Our story is that you are an Anglo horse trader he has done business with in the past. So do not speak to him of anything but horses when others may be listening, *comprende?"*

Longarm allowed that worked for him. They went on inside where Longarm was greeted with a formal bow by an older man who might not have had as much Indian blood as his daughter. But Don Jesus had enough, and it was likely Apache or Comanche, as he gravely said, *"Mi casa es su casa,* but I hope we understand that were you not . . . who you are, I would feel most obliged for to tear off your arms and legs, cut off your *pitón huevos* and shove them down your throat before I killed you, slowly?"

Longarm gravely replied, "There is no way for a true caballero to ask another true caballero why he feels that way unless he brings up the name of a third party neither wishes to speak of in a disrespectful manner. So I reckon I'll just never know what you're so het up about."

The older man laughed in spite of himself and turned to Pilar to say, "You were right. Now that I have met him I *do* like the gringo *chingado.* Why do we not offer him a drink as we wait for our *cena* to be served?"

Chapter 8

Poor Mexicans lived on tortillas and beans, or sometimes they served beans with tortillas for variety. Prosperous Mexicans, like prosperous Anglo Victorians, sat down to groaning boards to eat more than they likely should have in four- or five-course meals, soup to nuts. Longarm was glad he'd snacked earlier by the time the onion soup was seved after nine. But he was overstuffed before they finished up after ten. The main course was naturally roast pork. *Ricos* might have lamb or veal in season as a novelty. Longarm had long since suspected Mexicans of only serving hot tamales in front of Texas folk in an attempt to goad them into eating peppers. You never saw hot tamales nor chili con carne that peppersome as you got clear of the Tex-Mex border towns. There was hardly any pepper worth mention served that night at the high-toned Amendez spread.

After a dessert somebody had set on fire before carrying in from the kitchen, the gents retired to the smoking room whilst the ladies cleared *las mesas.* Knowing who'd be coming to dinner that night, Don Jesus had only invited his parish priest and a few other bigshots he hadn't cared to insult. None of them spoke much English to mention and when their host explained how *El Señor* Buck had ridden far on business they didn't seem to mind the two of them wandering on to a smaller study with their smokes and brandy glasses.

The cigars were Cuban and the brandy was Napoleon. As they settled in private near a cold fireplace, Longarm got to the business that had really brought him out that way.

Don Jesus had already heard about Chavez shearing all those so-called merinos before he'd delivered them. Longarm agreed it was sort of amusing and asked, "Are you saying the U.S. of A. didn't pay for true merinos?"

The local stockman soothed, "Nobody this side of old Spain has any true merinos. One might as well ask for the hand of *la enfanta* in marriage."

He took a drag on his claro and added, soothingly, "Only livestock not worthy of recorded ancestry on both sides was ever allowed to leave Spain for her colonies. But the stock Chavez sold your friends was as close to blue-blooded merino as one sees on this side of the main ocean. As in the case of our horses and cattle, is better for to have a little hardy *campesino* blood where the living is not so easy. The pure-enough merinos your government wishes for *los* Navahos will probably upgrade their herds to a creature that will give more wool without starving to death over in those canyonlands."

Longarm asked how come no Mexicans seemed to want to sign on with the BIA to deliver the infernal sheep.

The local Mexican shrugged and said, "None of us, how you say, have a dog in that fight. Is said that when the bulls fight, the chickens should stay out of the arena. Forgive me, I mean no offense, but you people are inclined to shoot at everyone in sight when you shoot it out."

"You think them Texas cattle folk off to the northwest mean to shoot it out with the U.S. government?" asked Longarm.

Don Jesus shrugged and said, "If they do, none of us wish for to be there. Over on the Pecos, just a few summers ago, some few of *La Raza* took sides when Major Murphy and his friends stood up to John Chisum and *his* friends.

Most of us did not. So most of us were still standing as the dust settled. Was a war to the death between lunatics. Dolan on one side and Chisum on the other came out alive but were worse off than before. Murphy, Brady, Tunstall, Brewer and McSween were all dead. For what? Who can say? Was not our fight. This business between your friends and those newcomers from Texas is not our fight. You shall have to have others herd those sheep across the mountains to *los* Navahos."

Longarm sipped some brandy and said, "I was hoping you might tell me more about how you'd go about that if you did care to help. To tell the truth, I've next to no idea how you run sheep across open range out this way."

The older man who dealt in all things agricultural along the upper Rio Grande, or Río Bravo, as he called it, waved his cigar expansively and pontificated, "Is no big secret. Is a business. To begin with six thousand sheep is spit in the ocean to a Mexican. A serious owner has perhaps six hundred thousand head under his majordomo, or *segundo*. The majordomo in turn parcels out the stock in manageble separate herds of say nine or ten thousand under riders called *caporales*. Each *caporal* has perhaps three or four vaqueros under him, *comprende*?"

Longarm frowned and said, "Not hardly. I've always understood a Mex vaquero to be a *cowboy*. What's a cowboy doing, herding sheep?"

Don Jesus looked pained and said, "When you people learned for how to graze stock on our sort of range you were not paying proper attention. To a *vaquero Mejicano* working stock is not a religious experience. I do not know where all this *mierda* about some code of some West comes from. The word, *vaquero*, you say *buckaroo*, means no more nor less than, let me see, I suppose you could translate it as "one who deals with *vaca*, cow," or for that matter any stock his patron wants him to. *El Vaquero* is a rider, and a good one, who tends the herds, the *mixed* herds of his patron. We do not see why you people only grow one crop in a cornfield, either. Anyone can tell you is more profitable to grow beans up cornstalks with peppers if not squash or melons growing between the corn rows. Around our smaller holdings or out across the range we graze what is best for what is there. In the rich *llanos* to the south of *Ciudad Méjico* one sees mixed herds of cattle, goats, pigs, sheep or even turkeys. Up this way is more better you herd sheep alone where the range is too sparse for anything else."

Longarm said, "That's what some cattle folk object to. But, all right, I'm with you as far as sheepherding vaqueros doing what?"

The Mexican explained, "What they do best. Riding the range, out ahead of the sheep to, how you say, scout for forage and, above all, water. A sheep can only live in a desert with help from its human friends. A sheep on its own can die of thirst with a water hole on the other side of a hill. A sheep is not a very intelligent animal."

Longarm said he'd long suspected as much.

The Mexican explained, "Each vaquero scouts for, directs and if need be, protects three or four *pastores* or shepherds, on foot. With the help of two or three dogs, each *pastore* herds a thousand to fifteen hundred sheep."

Longarm observed, "That's a heap of sheep for one man and a couple of dogs to handle, if you ask me."

Don Jesus shrugged and said, "Money is made or lost in raising stock according to how much one must spend raising it. *Pastores* are of course not paid as much as vaqueros and our vaqueros work for much less than your buckaroos. The numbers have been worked out over many years by many who raise sheep. A man or boy of average intelligence, assisted by dogs so much smarter than sheep, can hold a thousand head togther more often than not. When they can't, it's accepted as a natural loss. We do not grow each stalk of corn in a watered pot."

He smiled knowingly and added, "The sheep is only a little bit smarter than the cornstalk. Is a *crop*, not a *pet*. I do not understand how you people can hope to make money treating livestock as if it was related to you."

Longarm smiled thinly and said, "Lots of Anglo folk come out this way with more *hopes* than know-how. I recall this poor nester family I supped with up Montana way, one time, who'd planted apples on the prairie without asking how long it took for an apple tree to bear fruit."

Don Jesus smiled and said, "Not as bad as waiting for olive trees to bear, eh? I have read your Homestead Act. Was written by an idiot."

Longarm said, "Not if you could claim that quarter section back East where it rains some. The Pennsylvania Dutch thrive on eighty acres or so. The senators who figured twice that many acres ought to do for a family farm just never saw land where it took five acres of grazing for a single cow. But that is neither here nor there. They tell me one old boy who claims to be a sheepherder of the Scotch persuasion excused his failure to communicate with Mex merino sheep as a language problem."

The Mexican snorted and replied, "Nobody *talks* to *sheep* in any tongue. Sheepdogs are trained for to respond to simple whistled commands."

Longarm said, "This Scotsman, MacTavish, claims his dogs understand his Gaelic. Possible?"

The Mexican shrugged and decided, "I do not see what difference this would make to the sheep. Dogs do not speak to sheep. They turn them the other way by pretending to be coyotes."

Longarm decided, "MacTavish is likely what we call a grub-line rider, out for free meals and pocket jingle as a trail herd is forming up. I've seen old boys hang around a cow camp for weeks, that way, before time came to saddle up or shuffle on. Hard to tell how a man ropes or throws when there's no roping or throwing going on."

"Then you will expose this imposter when you go back to town?" asked the Mexican.

Longarm shrugged and said, "Ain't no fly in my soup. I

paid for my own education and old Dodsworth can pay for his. Got no call to tattle on a poor old boy who must be up against it."

"But you say the man is a liar!" insisted Don Jesus.

Longarm said, "He ain't lied to *me*, so far. When folk step on my toes I ask 'em to get off. Long as they treat me polite I feel no call to start up with them."

Don Jesus said, "You confuse me, *El Brazo Largo*. They say, one time, in old *Méjico*, you wiped out an army column with field artillery!"

To which Longarm could only reply, in a modest tone, "They stepped on my toes. I just hate it when *Los Federales* come after an old boy who's just trying to do his job."

The older man nodded and said, "I am beginning to see why you have so many friends in spite of your reputation for ferocity. I can see why my daughter seems so fond of you."

He took a healthy sip of brandy before he continued in a firmer tone, "My daughter has proven herself a woman with a mind of her own and her mother and I have learned to accept this. So what happens in town is what happens in town. But I hope you understand that should it happen out here under my roof I shall feel it in my toes?"

Longarm allowed they understood one another right well and so before midnight he was riding back to town, alone, with a wistful hard-on, but that was the way a heap of swell dinner parties were inclined to end.

As he rode along in the moonlight he reflected on his conversation with a man who knew his sheep from sheep shit and decided things might not be as complexicated as he'd feared. He already knew how to scout on ahead of fodder, water or worse. If those replacement sheepherders came with trained dogs they'd run 'em spread out in half a dozen flocks one man and his dogs could manage. If not, they could likely herd 'em like cows, as Gluepants Gafferty had suggested. So the real question before the house was how they were going to get those cattle outfits to stand to one side and let 'em pass.

He left Dancer in the hotel stable, his saddle in the tack room, and went on upstairs with his saddlebags and Winchester. The stairwell and top story hall were dimly lit by candle sconces. But as he approached his hired room he could see the match stem on the hall runner, which was not where he'd left it locking up. Some sneak had tripped his simple burglar alarm when they'd opened the door to dislodge the match stem Longarm had wedged under the bottom hinge.

He tried the knob gingerly. The door wasn't locked. He took a deep breath, kicked the door open and followed the muzzle of his Winchester in after the whirling saddlebags he'd flung into the dark ahead of them.

As he'd hoped, he heard a thud and somebody gasping in surprised discomfort. Then Longarm was all over that somebody and as the two of them landed on the rug he got a good grip on one tit and growled, "Move one muscle and you're dead, you bastard!"

Then he felt the tit he was grasping more thoughtfully as he sat astride the form he'd flattened and decided, "Sorry, ma'am, I thought you were somebody else."

To which she replied in an icy hiss, "I know who you thought I was, goddamn you! But I'm not Judith Morrison and you're not Latigo Shaw, so who in the name of sweet reason might you be, you lying moose?"

Letting go her tit, but hanging on to his Winchester, Longarm fished out a waterproof match and thumbnailed it alight to stare down in wonder at the woman he'd pinned to the floor. Her hat had flown off and her sun-bleached flaxen hair lay spread out across the rug as her gray eyes blazed up at him like gun muzzles fixing to fire. As he took in her still-handsome but weathered features Longarm added everything up to decide, "Miss Marmion MacEwen, I presume?"

She hissed, "Who were you expecting, as if I didn't know? And why did you tell her you were Latigo Shaw?"

71

"Ain't I Latigo Shaw?" was the best he could come up with.

The blond gal sneered up at him to demand, "If you are Latigo Shaw, who did I just send packing, up in Denver?"

Chapter 9

That struck Longarm as a good question. So he got off her and rose to apply the flickering wax-stemmed match to a bed lamp before it burned down to his fingers. Then he put the Winchester on the bed table, left the saddlebags where they lay and helped the lady to her feet before he stepped around her to shut the hall door.

When he turned to face her some more she was holding a Schofield .45 in one dainty fist, trained on his chest. He sighed and said, "Serves me right for trusting a woman. But if you shoot me I'll never speak to you again, Miss Marmion."

She almost smiled and repeated her question as to his identity.

He replied, "How do you like my being Buck Crawford, out of work and looking to hire on with the Bureau of Indian Affairs?"

She said, "You'll have to do better than that. That hotheaded Judith Morrison says she fell in with you aboard the night train from Denver and knew right away who you were. So you were feeding her a line of bull long before you got here to Albuquerque."

Then she asked, hopefully, "Run that part about Indian Affairs past me again."

73

Longarm said, "That's who'd amassed all them sheep, over in the yards, as a distraction to the Navaho nation. Hasn't old Ed Dodsworth been saying as much all over town?"

She replied, "Of course. But everyone's assumed he was lying. I'll have you know I'm not in *favor* of sheep pushing out across our cattle range like wooly locusts. But I lost a husband I was fond of to a range war down in West Texas and when Judith boasted she'd set up a meeting with a hired gun I got there first and paid him good money to go back to Cheyenne and just forget the whole thing."

She let that sink in and added, "So you can imagine how I felt when I heard he, or somebody like him, had come on down to take up arms against that . . . You're not funning me about it really being an Indian Agency outfit?"

He said, "On my word, as an enlisted man, ma'am. You and your friends have nothing to fear if you let them sheep pass on by. And, as you just suggested, you could be asking for more than a range war if you fire on officials of the U.S. government!"

She lowered the muzzle of her old thumb buster as he relentlessly went on, "Bureau of Indian Affairs rides for the Secretary of the Interior, old Carl Schurz. Secretary Schurz runs Land Management with another set of books. The books your homestead claims are registered in, if you follow my drift."

She did. Holstering her six-gun she gasped, "This is worse than I feared! I know how such feuds can take everybody down with them! Less than half the cattle outfits over to McKinley County voted to make a stand against those sheepherders. But the ones who did voted to make her a fight to the finish. What, oh what, are we to ever do?"

Longarm said, "My own notion was to simply convince everybody there was nothing to fight about. Nobody means to graze sheep permanent on your open range, Miss Marmion."

She repressed a shudder and said, "Some of them are never going to believe that. Some of them don't *want* to believe that."

She bent to pick up her hat and, as long as she was down that way, got those saddlebags as well. Some women were just tidy by nature and a man had to watch out for 'em. Lest they make him wear a necktie.

Neatly folding the saddlebags over the foot of his hired bed, she put her hat back on to complete her rough and ready riding costume. Then she sighed and said, "I remember how it was when my big brothers rode off to join Hood's Brigade during the war between the states. My folks pleaded with 'em to stay out of it. We were cattle folk. Had no darkies working for us, free or bound. They still rode off to the war and neither came back. I married up with a neighbor boy who did. He'd been wounded twice and swore he'd never take up arms against any white man and he tried to keep his word on that."

Longarm didn't ask what had happened to her man. He knew she'd tell him. She looked away and said, "He tried to stay out of it. He really did. But when you don't take sides both sides are inclined to think you must be on the other side. We never found out which side gunned him as he rode alone out by one of our own tanks."

Longarm soberly said, "I've had this same conversation with responsible adults, red, white and in between. I suspect it's our own fault. I mean the fault of those who've lived through troubled times. We tend to talk about things long after the gunsmoke fades away and as we talk the kids who weren't there get to feeling left out. So by the time they're big enough to go to war you just can't tell 'em they never missed all that much. So each generation gets to learn the hard way.

"I was just reading in the *Illustrated Police Gazette* how that young widow of Louis Napoleon keeps calling on a new generation of Frenchmen to avenge the beating they took in that Franco-Prussian War by going another round with them."

He grimaced and added, "She's got to keep the home fires burning. I suspect the next big war they have over yonder will be worse. But when the bugles blow and the drums start drumming you'll no doubt find plenty of French and Prussian kids raring to go."

He got out his notebook and added, "Long as we're on the subject, and seeing you're in a better position to know, I could use a list of the hotheads we'll be up against, Miss Marmion."

She blanched and protested, "You can't ask me to betray my own kind to a *stranger*, ah, Buck."

He said, "You may as well know I'm more than a stranger. I'm the law. Federal. Riders who take on the federal government ain't your own kind unless your own kind is *loco en la cabeza*. They're fixing to rob your own kind of your homestead claims, water rights, grazing rights and any other rights you all think you have out yonder by right of wood and water."

She smiled uncertainly and asked, "You know about those pagan customs of a Celtic past, Buck?"

He said, "I read about 'em. I wasn't there. The history of your old Scotch Highlands might not have been so exciting if everybody had followed one set of rules. But they never did. Some of them clan chiefs held title to feudal holdings under their high king in Perth, or up in Sweden, as they saw fit to decide for their fool selves."

She sighed and said, "You're leaving out the Lord Of the Islands."

He said, "Whatever. A whole bunch of the smaller clans, adding up to a whole lot of feuding and fussing, held that land belonged by natural law to them who'd first gathered firewood and drinking water on the same. It sounds sensible enough, until you try to clear title with the county clerk. On this side of the water we call such claims *squatting* and if you can hold your claim seven years against all comers the courts may uphold your title. But don't bet on it if you get Little Big Eyes sore at you."

"Little who?" she marveled.

He said, "Secretary of the Interior Carl Schurz, born a German but wound up a Union general, a senator and a party boss. He's currently in charge of the Interior Department, as I mentioned earlier, under his old pal, President Hayes, and you mess with him at your peril."

She protested, "*I* don't want to mess with anybody. I believe what you say about those sheep. They're welcome to water and graze on my Double W. But you have to understand how some of my kind feel outraged by the mere thought of *sheep* on *cattle* range!"

He said, "I understand. I told you I read. I know all about the sacred cows of the pagan Aryan tribes and I agree them Highland clearances were enough to make a lot of Christians feel bad about sheep. But we ain't talking about sheep grazing grass reserved for sacred cows. The open range of these United States is grazed by permit of the Land Management Office of the U.S., Department of the Interior and, if said office so desires, that open range can be grazed by two-humped camels or spotted giraffes with a hillside snorter thrown in."

She dimpled and said, "Silly, there's no such critter as a hillside snorter!"

To which he soberly replied, "The Land Office can still issue a grazing permit for one, if it so desires. Just as it can *bar* any species of stock with a stroke of the pen. You can trust me on this because I had to enforce such an order up Wyoming way when this big cattle outfit insisted it had the right to cross Indian lands, cutting fences as it did so."

He wasn't certain she believed him, so he continued, "The land office ain't got the time nor the manpower to keep tabs on all its open range. Wild stock as well as buffalo and pronghorn wander at will where nobody cares. But if you get anybody in Washington *caring*, like I said, they can shut you down with a stroke of a pen and if you don't like it, that's where federal men like me come in."

She started to cry.

He said, "Aw, mush, we got days, mayhaps as long as a week, to sell Miss Judith and her bunch on standing aside as them sheep get delivered. I've been trying to get Dodsworth to drive *around* you all across Indian lands to the south. We got plenty of time to plot a peaceable solution. So about that list of names you were fixing to give me . . ."

She lowered her lashes to murmur, "I don't know. How do I know I can trust you, Buck?"

He thought hard, nodded, and said, "You're right. It ain't right to fib to a fellow plotter. You already knew I wasn't the real Latigo Shaw, but let's keep that our own little secret for now. I ain't Buck Crawford, either. I'd be Deputy U.S. Marshal Custis Long, assigned to shotgun them sheep on through to Standing Rock, come hell or high water."

She gasped, "I've heard of you! The Mexicans say you once wiped out a Mexican army column! They call you *El Brazo Largo,* or Longarm, right?"

He muttered, "Serves me right for not keeping my big mouth shut. I want your word you'll keep my true name a secret, Miss Marmion."

She said, "Of course. But why? Wouldn't it be easier to convince Judith Morrison and her faction they were looking for trouble if we told them who you were and who you were working for?"

He said, "It would, if they believed me. Like you said, for some fool reason some of them ain't willing to believe what Dodsworth has been telling everybody since he and his staff got here. He bought them sheep with an Interior Department draft on a local bank. Every Mexican I've talked to seems to believe Dodsworth's tale of woe. I'm still working on why Miss Judith and some hard-core holdouts keep insisting it's all a plot to infest their range with a permanent plague."

She opined, "Judith has always been mighty spoiled. Her uncle Donald doted on her when he was alive and since she inherited the Rocking M and a bunkhouse full of hardcase Texas hairpins she's become impossible to talk sense to."

He said, "She reminds me of that French Empress who wants to start up with the Prussians some more. My original plan was to string her along as a pet hired gun and *let her figure out* the simple truth. Why don't you think that might work?"

The older cattle woman said, "I don't like that notion. I don't think she and the hotheads she's preening for *want* the truth. I think they want to fight, with or without just cause."

She looked away as she added, "After that, I don't think I like the notion of you fooling around with Judith Morrison."

He took a step toward her without thinking too far ahead. She flinched away and protested, "I never said I wanted anybody fooling with *me* that way!"

"The thought never crossed my mind," Longarm lied.

She blushed and stammered, "Honestly, you let a man feel you up a tad by accident and the next thing you know he's all over you!"

Longarm assured her, "I ain't out to seduce you, Miss Marmion. I only want you to help me head off a needless shoot-out."

So they sat side by side on the bed as she spelled out the troubled souls she feared he'd have to watch for if he tried to drive sheep across the public lands of McKinley County.

They added up to nigh a platoon of riders she had down as mean and dumb enough to do most anything a willful she-boss told them to, with as many more undecided and likely to swing either way as they judged the odds. *Nobody* over in McKinley County *liked* sheep, sheepherders or, for that matter, the U.S. government. Some of the older riders had fought for Texas during the war. Many of the younger

79

ones were itching for a chance to pot a greaser, a nigger or a damnyankee, and you had to take such brags seriously.

Texas boys such as John Wesley Hardin and King Fisher had been known to gun most anyone they listed as fair game for no good reason at all. A tale was told of a Texas tough, his name varied with the telling, who'd gunned a colored cavalryman in cold blood, observing it was an insult to a noble steed to let a monkey or a nigger ride it. Before he'd managed to bust his own fool neck, up Cimarron way, an unreconstructed rebel called Clay Allison had shot three colored soldiers just for entering the same taproom. Given an *excuse* to prey on what they regarded as lesser breeds, such unreconstructed rebels could be real pains in the ass. Longarm considered singling out one of the rowdier young gun hands on the list and making an example of him. But that could lead a lawman down a slippery slope indeed. There was little to be said for a lawman who hunted other men to make examples of them, as if he were collecting trophy heads.

Once he had a list of hairpins to watch out for, Longarm had no call to stop Marmion MacEwen when she got up to leave. She told him how she was staying, it turned out, there at the same hotel for the night. As he let her out, there came an awkward moment with the two of them in the doorway, enveloped in the warm fumes of her toilet water and she-sweat.

He didn't ask if she knew her toilet water smelled like raspberries. It seemed an odd choice, but she likely knew. He felt like kissing her. He sensed she wanted him to kiss her. But he never did and they parted with a handshake.

So it hardly seemed fair, at breakfast the next morning, when that fool Indian agent, Dodsworth, smiled slyly at him to remark, "I must say I admire your taste, ah, Buck. I was coming from the latrine last night when you let that stunning blonde out of your own room, you dog, you!"

Longarm shook his head and said, "That wasn't the way

things was. The lady you saw was more like a government witness, see?"

Dodsworth laughed and lightly replied, "Anything you say, Don Juan. I'd want to keep anything that fine all to myself as well. I swear a woman like that could inspire a duel and . . . she's not been spoken for in these parts, has she?"

To which Longarm could only reply, "I sure hope not."

Chapter 10

As others working with Dodsworth drifted into the hotel dining room the only one there in the know kept introducing Longarm as Hick Crawford, a cattleman and former army scout with some knowlege of the Navaho and the Four Corners canyon country. As Longarm and Dodsworth had already agreed, it wasn't as important to keep their fellow federal employees in the dark as it was to preserve the illusion he was a hired gun spying on them for Judith Morrison and her determined opposition.

Two could keep a secret when one of them was dead and Longarm had been forced to let all too many in on a secret that could get him killed if the wrong rascal tumbled to it.

Dodsworth's junior agents, Roberts and Tanner, seemed all-purpose ration clerks. Neither had ever been west of the Mississippi before.

Agent Roberts seemed content to keep his mouth shut and his ears open. But Agent Tanner wanted it known he understood Indians and larded his speech with heap-big-cigar-store Indian jargon. Longarm managed not to smile when Tanner asked about Navaho squaws weaving blankets in their wigwams. But it wasn't easy.

He knew he'd sound like a know-it-all if he lectured

them on one of the most difficult lingos on Earth. So he left Tanner to his blissful ignorance for the time being.

An older cuss called Arnold Hoffmann was introduced as an expert on sheep, on loan from the Department of Agriculture. Longarm thought old Hoffmann looked more like an old goat than a sheep. But he never said so.

The five of them were lighting up over their coffee and empty plates when they were joined by three more from the nearby lobby. Dodsworth's two remaining hired herders, MacTavish and DuVille, had been talking with Reporter Phalen from the *Santa Fe Weekly Democrat* when the three of them had spied the gathering in the dining room and ambled in for some coffee. All three had eaten earlier that morning.

Reporter Phalen looked to be in his late thirties and sounded as if he knew his way around New Mexico Territory. DuVille was a quiet young French Canadian. Hamish MacTavish was a ruddy-faced and red-bearded cuss who looked like he was bullshitting you with his mouth shut.

Longarm knew Scots who hadn't been evicted to make room for sheep had been hired as sheepherders and some were said to be good at it. Hamish MacTavish implied he was even better, sounded like a music hall comic and he was wearing—for Chrissake—kilts. Longarm was reminded of that wry definition of the kilt as a garment that was most often worn in Scotland by Americans and in America by Scots. It wasn't easy. But Longarm managed not to ask MacTavish if he'd spent much time in cactus country with his bow legs so bare.

Once the introductions were out of the way, Longarm deemed it a good time to bring all assembled up-to-date on his conversation with Don Jesus, regarding sheep, not daughters.

Young DuVille allowed the Mex methods sounded sensible to him, even though he'd never herded more than five hundred head at a time, himself. MacTavish said they ranged flocks of five thousand over the hills and dales of the Highlands back home.

Dodsworth decided, "We'll need more riders, ah, Buck. If you ride out ahead as the . . . *caporal*, then Tanner, Roberts, Mister Hoffmann, here and myself will only be able to act as vaqueros for four out of six of our thousand-head flocks. So we need two more riders along with four more herdsmen and their dogs, right?"

MacTavish said, "Ye'd better let me ride as a buckaroo, ye ken As I told ye before, I've been having trouble wi' me collies. Had I noo raised them me ownself I'd swear they'd been switched aboard the steamer!"

Dodsworth replied, "I thought you said your dogs were fine but Mexican sheep didn't understand them."

MacTavish looked thunderghasted and demanded, "When might I ha' said a loony like sae? Och, I fear me brogue confuses e'ryone. Dogs dinna talk to sheep. Sheep canna understand any speech. Wha' I meant to say . . ."

"Never mind," Dodsworth cut in, turning back to Longarm to continue, "Wherever we assign Mr. MacTavish and his confused collies, I take it we're planning to drive those Mexican merinos to Standing Rock in the Mexican manner?"

Longarm replied, "I've been going over the survey maps some more. I make her roughly a hundred miles from here to Standing Rock. But you don't drive stock in beelines over semiarid rugged range, with or without most of the way disputed. You have to zig and zag for grazing and even wider for water. You have to scout for bedding grounds like they tell about in the Good Book. Sheep are easier to hold overnight in green pastures beside the still waters."

Young DuVille piped up, "Forgive me, I may be missing something. I only know the sort of scenery you have out here from my cross-country ride aboard the trains. *Mais* if this hundred miles you speak of is as barren and rough as a lot of range I have seen so far, we are speaking of a very long and dusty trail, *non*?"

Longarm said, "You ain't seen nothing yet. The trains run through more sensible stretches where the grading don't cost 'em as much. Betwixt here and Standing Rock the grade climbs considerable, with wet and dry washes to cross. Such grazing as there might be is scattered wide and, like I said, our route is disputed by unreconstructed rebels who worship cows."

He let that sink in and went on, "Eight or ten miles a day would be too much to hope for, driving direct across that disputed hilly range. I defer to any man here about the herding of sheep. But I do have more than one suggestion, based on the little I do know."

Nobody there tried to stop him.

Longarm said, "The route to the northwest really zig-zags one hundred and, say, fifty miles, which is one hell of a way for any man to trudge on *foot* in this climate. A pro-fessional bronc buster I met tells me sheep can be driven like small fuzzy cows for reasonable distances by herders on horseback."

Hoffmann, from Agriculture, objected, "Sheep can't trot that fast and they need to browse more often than cattle."

Longarm said, "A horse can walk slow as a man if you don't spur it. Meanwhile, a man with his ass in the saddle sweats a whole lot less and can go a whole lot farther than a man on foot. The riders will have to trot more, cutting off strays and such. But they can move the sheep at a steady mile-eating pace, letting them break trail to graze when-ever or wherever they come across greenery worth grazing. I don't expect water to be such a problem this early in the year, driving across high range. So we're talking about, say, two weeks on the trail and what if we went for three?"

Dodworth sniffed, "You're not going to bring that alter-nate route to the south up again, I hope!"

Longarm said, "Hope springs eternal and I hope you'll pay more attention this time. If I could scout up some riders who ain't afraid of sheep we could start this very afternoon and be down to the crossing into BIA Reserve by sundown. I know that route will cost us as long as another week on the trail. Are you expecting those extra sheepherders to get here any sooner?"

Dodsworth shook his head and replied, "Perhaps not. But the government has contracted for them and as we speak they are on their way! How would it look in Washington if we left four professional drivers and their dogs stranded here in Albuquerque with no sheep to herd and no place to go but back East, at government expense?"

Old Hoffmannn huffed, "Our travel orders are all down on paper. There's no way to change them at this late date, even if we agreed with your alternate route, which I, for one, do not. When you plan a government project you're supposed to follow it through as laid out!"

Longarm sipped some coffee before he morosely mused, "That's what they say, sure enough. But once upon a time there was this Union general. They called him Little Mac and put him in command of the army of the Potomac because he was a thundering wonder when it came to putting plans down on paper."

Reporter Phalen asked if he was talking about General George McClellan.

Longarm nodded and replied, George B. graduated near the top of his class and served all over creation with distinction as a military attaché and peacetime garrison commander. I have a saddle he invented out in the tack room and it's a pisser, with every last detail worked out scientific by a born nitpicker who just loved military science."

He gave them time to consider as he sipped more coffee. Then he went on, "The soldiers who served under him loved Little Mac like a father because he led them beside still waters and made them lie down in green pastures. He was a born bookkeeper who never made a mistake, on paper; every man in his command was fully equipped head to toe. His Army of the Potomac never missed a meal and his field kitchens served the best army grub known to man. He inspected the shit out of his troops to make sure they all had the regulation number of bullets to go with their spit-and-polish Springfields. He had, in sum, the best damned troops the U.S. Army had ever put in the field."

Reporter Phalen, who was old enough to recall, said, "Then came the battle of Antietam."

Longarm nodded and said, "It did indeed, and it was the bloodiest battle of the whole war, with the cream of the Union Army slugging it out toe-to-toe with best troops of the Confederacy, Lee's Army of Virginia."

Dodsworth, who was also old enough to remember, sniffed and said, "The Union won, of course."

Longarm nodded and said, "Sure it did. It had to. They had the numbers as well as some damned fine training on their side. Lee's men were good. They cut the oncoming Yankees down in windrows, but they couldn't stop 'em and rebel blood was flowing like water along the Bloody Lane by the time the Army of Virginia broke and ran for its life."

Dodsworth asked, "What has the Battle of Antietam to do with our herding sheep to Standing Rock?"

Longarm said, "Government planning as can't be changed or modified. Neither Little Mac nor Robert E. could see all that was going on, of course. But as the sun was setting aides were telling Lee his whole army was in retreat. At the same time other aides were telling McClellan much the same. His junior officeres *wanted* to seize the initiative and shove Lee's shattered army to Virginia and beyond. They likely could have. Soldiers on the run with no orders tend to just keep running. But McClellan ordered a full field inspection of the troops he had left before he moved 'em from where they were still standing as the gunsmoke cleared."

He sipped more coffee, sighed, and said, "That was the way a careful planner who went by the book was supposed to do it. He took his time to make certain there were more dead rebs than boys in blue. Then he issued fresh ammunition, dressed up the ranks with replacements to have every company back up to full strength, and allowed it was time to start the war again. Once he had, he discoved Bobby Lee had gathered up his shattered army, formed them up again as best he could manage, playing it by ear, and the war got started again indeed."

He could see from the looks passed between the government officials that he hadn't made his point. So he finished his coffee without offering McClellan's replacement, General Unconditional Surrender Grant, as his own notion of a rough-and-ready field commander. He had to allow, to be fair, Grant had been a hell of a general but a disappointment as a president because there were times to buckle down to the books and times to just roll with the punches. He knew they'd want to keep records as to the profits and losses of an upgraded herd once they got the blamed sheep to the blamed Navaho. But they had to *get* them there before they carded and spun any wool!

Reporter Phalen hesitated, then said, "I was sent down here to report the news, not to create it. But for what my opinion is worth, all this talk about driving sheep anywhere on horseback is moot."

He nodded at the BIA men and continued firmly but not unkindly, "A ride in the park is one thing. Driving stock aboard a cutting pony is another. You'd need at least a score of damned good drovers to move six thousand head of anything any number of miles and the word's gone out, gentlemen. You're simply not going to hire a score of Mex or Anglo riders in these parts of New Mexico Territory."

"Who put out said word?" asked Longarm, as if he couldn't guess.

The local newspaper man shrugged and replied, "Who put out the word in Lincoln County back in '78? A hundred years from now they'll still be trying to fix the blame. As such tensions build some bolt their doors and crawl under the covers while others circle in like wolves sniffing the wind. Suffice to say word's gone out that the powers that be over in McKinley County are determined to stand their ground and won't take kindly to anybody they may or may not know riding for the other side."

Dodsworth protested, "But the other side is their own government! How can they hope to win a shoot-out with their own government?"

Phalen smiled thinly and pointed out, "A lot of their more experienced gun hands learned their craft riding for Texas against their own government. Back in '78, with the shoe on the other foot, a handful of outsiders decided to go up against an established clique of army officers, retired or still active, who'd been running New Mexico Territory for thirty years. History would be less interesting if everybody behaved with common sense."

Dodsworth insisted, "This is—damn it—not the same sort of situation as they had in Lincoln County. Nobody is out to take over McKinley County."

Phalen shrugged and said, "The cattle interest running McKinley County may not feel they're in charge if they have to stand aside and let others have their way. I'm sure most of them have to know, deep down inside, that nobody is out to raise sheep forever on their range. But they've drawn their line in the sand and when a bully boy backs down he loses the Indian sign he's had on everyone else in his neck of the woods."

"It's stupid! They're risking everything they have, if not their very lives, on a point of schoolyard honor!"

Phalen shrugged and murmured, "You're right. The new governor, old Bible-thumping Lew Wallace, has already sent word he'll come down on them like a ton of bricks if they start another range war on him. Ever hear of an educated lawyer called Aaron Burr? He'd made it to vice president of these United States when he threw it all away in an affair of honor and I can't say much for Alexander Hamilton's brains that morning, either. Men who take to settling arguments with guns don't always think too far ahead."

Dodsworth said, "If those crazy cowboys gun one of

our party, or for that matter any of our sheep, they stand to wind up flat broke in a federal prison. Don't you see it that way, ah, Buck?"

To which Longarm could only reply, "When you're right, you're right. But when you're dead, you're dead, no matter what they do to the other son of a bitch."

Chapter 11

Dodsworth caught Longarm alone at the Western Union office closer to the railroad station. Longarm had just wired a progress report, such as he'd made, to his home office. Dodsworth said he was there to do much the same and, whilst he was at it, see if he could build a fire under them to get those extra sheepherders out their way.

As they stood in the doorway, with Longarm facing out, he spotted that big Mex sombrero with the scrawny kid under it. The *muchacho* was hunkered on his heels with his back braced against the adobe wall of a sideyard on the shady side of the street, just out of easy pistol range.

Longarm said, "Don't look now. But one of us is being followed. As an educated guess, I'd say it was me. After that it gets murksome. Judith Morrison's faction knows where I am. I told her where I'd be. The peace party Marmion MacEwen rides with knew where I could be found when she found me last night. I shook that kid off before I dined with Don Jesus last night. I wonder what the little piss ant's waiting for me to do. Would you care to help me catch him so's we could mayhaps find out?"

Dodsworth asked what he had in mind.

Longarm said, "He's been put on my tail, not yours. Why don't you send your own wires to Washington whilst I have a smoke, here? After both of us are free to move faster, I'll sashay off up the tracks as if to see how them sheep are doing. You stay here in the shade and just watch until the kid unglues his shirt from that wall to tail me some more. You let him tail me 'til he's just in sight with his back to you. Then you tail him 'til all of us are over in the rail yards and I'll see if I can get him to follow me along one of them narrow lanes betwixt the blocks of stock pens."

He gave Dodworth time to get the picture and added, "I don't need to look back. He'll have no call to suspect I'm on to him before I get to the far end to stop and just double back on the little shit. He'll run from me, right into you. How do you like it so far?"

Dodsworth hesitated before he asked, "What if he's armed? How do we explain it if I wind up *hurting* somebody's darling boy?"

Longarm shrugged and asked, "How do you know there ain't a big black booger hiding under your bed? The kid can't be twelve years old and he's bare of foot and wearing no more than peon cotton under that expensive hat he found somewheres. But let it go. I'll catch him some other way, if he doesn't chop me up with that battle axe he's packing."

Dodsworth protested, "I never said I wouldn't. I just need some time to take this all in. I'm not a violent man, ah, Buck. I wanted to sign up for the war but they said I'd be more useful to them supervising an Indian school. At the Shinnecock Agency on Long Island."

Longarm soberly replied, "You must have done a fine job. I don't recall a Shinnecock uprising during the war."

"Don't mock me! I'll do it!" the older man protested, moving inside as he added, "Just let me send my own damned wires, first."

So Longarm stood by and lit a cheroot as the BIA man flustered over his form with a pencil. As he handed his message in to the telegraph clerk Dodsworth told Longarm he'd asked them for more backup.

Longarm said, "You got all the backup they aim to give you, namely, me. They told me what you were up against before they sent me down here to back you and nothing's changed all that much."

Before the BIA man could cloud up and rain all over him, Longarm told him, "You gotta understand the manpower situation out our way, pard. The West might not be so wild if there were less open space and more folk to fill it. But that ain't the way it is. The way it is has a sheriff and a half dozen deputies trying to police counties the size of Ireland. As we speak Victorio and no more than a mounted platoon of Bronco Apache have most of our Army of the West busy chasing them. That ain't as silly as it sounds when you consider how small our Army of the West happens to be. Small numbers add up to big doings out our way. The James-Younger gang has never put a dozen men in the saddle at one time. That Lincoln County War that's still echoing in these parts was fought by, say, a dozen riders under Dick Brewer, riding for the Tunstall-McSween-Chisum faction and a larger if less organized bunch deputized on and off by the Murphy-Dolan machine. When the powers that be had had enough they sent away to Fort Stanton for a military detchment with an old field gun or a gatling gun, depending on your reporter. Reports of Susan McSween playing her piano as the big guns blazed are bullshit. All the women on the premises left before the shooting started. Once troops arrived in serious numbers it was good as over."

Dodsworth chortled, "Then if we had one troop of cavalry backing us as we drove west . . ."

"You won't," Lonagm cut in, adding, "They send in the troops after a lot of folk get killed, not before. In a land of little rain and lots of wind the powers that be are betting on more wind than rain. If we get shot up bad Governor Wallace will declare Martial Law and warn both sides he means to hang the next rascal who fires a shot. If that don't work he *might* call troops back from chasing Apache. Or he might not be as worried about us as Apache. If you still mean to go on, we'd best find out who that Mex kid's working for. Don't break cover until he has his back to you. Let's do it."

Without waiting for an answer Longarm stepped out into the brighter light, gripping his cheroot at a jaunty angle with his teeth, and strode up First Street past the railroad station before cutting over to the cinder-paved service road that was some fifty feet closer to the rail yards. He ambled along at what he hoped that kid would take as his natural pace, knowing the shorter-legged kid would have to pick 'em up and lay 'em down too often to glance back the way he'd come. Longarm never glanced back. He knew Dodsworth was tailing them both or Dodsworth was a shit, and this was as good a time as any to find out.

He passed the bleating penned-up sheep. It took a spell. Then he came to the end of their block of pens and swung east, closer to the tracks as he scouted without appearing to. A man could take in a lot from under a hat brim without turning his head.

He spied what looked good enough and headed into it as if he had some destination in mind. A long, nearly solid row of railroad toolsheds ran betwixt the rail yards and the stockyards, with a narrow cinder path betwixt the board and baton sheds and the horizonal rails of another block of stock pens. In this case, the pens were empty save for a couple of cows near the far end where cattle stood despondent in the midmorning sun.

Longarm ambled on past the lowing cows until he came to the last pen. Then he turned on a dime to see that scrawny kid stammer to an awkward halt under his big hat.

As Longarm headed back toward him, the kid spun round to run, only to see the slightly shorter but way wider form of Dodsworth blocking his way. So, without hesitation, the kid rolled out from under his hat through the rails of the nearest cattle pen and tore through the longhorns like a determined butting billy goat, parting them like the red sea as he called back, "*Chinga tu madre, El Brazo Largo!*"

Then all that was left was a mocking rooster laugh as the milling cows hid the *muchacho* from view.

As Dodsworth joined Longarm he gasped, "We'll never catch him, now! What was that he yelled at us?"

Longarm was smiling as he said, "He was yelling it at me. He advised me to be very rude to my dear old mother, addressing me by a name I am seldom called on this side of the border. Let's go back to the telegraph office. I got to argue a point of company policy with Western Union."

Everybody learned in school how Sam Morse had invented the electric telegraph. A better businessman named Ezra Cornell had invented making money at it. Before he'd died stinking rich in '74, old Ezra had laid out a heap of rules and regulations designed to keep his customers coming back for more. One iron-bound rule had been that nobody, ever, got to read the private messages sent by others.

Longarm allowed he never wanted to set old Ezra to spinning in his grave but, seeing how many miles of Western Union wire ran across federal open range, it might be best to split some differances.

So, in the end, he was able to establish that, yes, a person or persons the clerk was not at liberty to disclose had sent a message that was none of Longarm's business to the *Rurales* barracks south of the El Paso border crossing a day earlier.

Longarm thanked the telegrapher sincere and lit a three-for-a-nickel cheroot for him, allowing he could guess the rest.

Then he sent another wire to his Denver office, explaining to Dodsworth, "My boss, Marshal Billy Vail, can cut a trail along telegraph wires as keenly as a bloodhound with its nose to wet ground. Somebody up this way who knows how bad some still want me down that way has recognized me and wired home for money. They had that kid tailing me with a view to out-of-town bounty hunters wanting to know just where I might be, once they get here by rail."

Dodsworth asked, "What are you going to do about that? Stake out the railroad station?"

Longarm said, "Might work, against bush leaguers. If I was on my way to get off a train in old Mexico with my Anglo face hanging out I reckon I'd get off at another stop and ease on in from some other direction."

Then he brightened and added, "That kid's careless taunt gives me an edge I didn't have a few minutes ago. I know who's after me. I could have have gone on suspecting Judith Morrison's faction might be on to me."

As they walked back to their hotel, Dodsworth asked about the next move he planned against that bunch.

Longarm said, "I ain't working *against* 'em. I'm out to save 'em a heap of trouble. We've established I've wiggle-wormed my way in to your outfit. I reckon it's time I rode out to that Rocking M to confide what I've found out about you."

"What are you going to tell them about us?" asked Dodsworth, warily.

Longarm said, "The simple truth. Now that I've made certain you all plan no more than a one-way drive to Standing Rock. I'll tell her I held off on shooting any of you before I made sure she still wanted me to."

"Gee, thanks," chuckled Dodsworth.

At the hotel entrance they shook where everyone within pistol range could see them doing it. Then Longarm walked around to the back alley to see about saddling Dancer up for some hard riding. It was close to twenty miles northwest to where the home spread of the Rocking M stood on the far side of that Rio Puerco. They'd likely named it long ago for the wild javelinas rooting at the willow roots, looking close enough to *puercos* or pigs.

Before he made the stable door, a shadowy figure detached itself from the shade across the alley to say, "Boss lady wants a word with you, mister . . . Jesus H. Christ!"

Longarm kept the .44-40 he'd drawn aimed right where it figured to do the most harm as he replied, "Don't ever pop out of nowhere like so at a man with a gun, pilgrim. Who's the boss lady we're talking about?"

The husky, somewhat younger, cowhand he had the drop on stammered, "I ride for Miss Judith of the Rocking M. You can call me Slats and I heard you rode for her as well. Where the hell did you ever learn to draw like that Mr. . . . Crawford?"

Longarm said, "That's what I told her I'd tell those sheepherders, Slats. She should have told you I can't afford to be slow on the draw in my line of work. Is she here in town? I was just fixing to ride out to the Rocking M. I got some words for her as well."

Slats said, "Miss Judith has a town house here in Albuquerque. She stays here overnight when she has beeswax in the city. Our home spread lies twenty miles out."

Longarm allowed he'd noticed as he put his six-gun away. He had his double derringer palmed in his other fist if the stranger tried anything sneaky.

Slats didn't. He led the way down to Copper Avenue and they followed it towards the old town a quarter mile to where a typical casa wrapped around a patio. Another Anglo cowhand lounged in the archway with his sawed off double-barrel ten-guage cradled in his arms. Slats howdied him and they strode on by to where Judith Morrison was seated at a garden table near a trickling fountain under a grape arbor.

As Longarm strode over to her he noticed there was no other chair. Judith glanced up at him, a cool vision in a summer frock with her long black hair let down. But when he smiled at her she blazed, "You're in on it with them, aren't you?"

Longarm smiled down uncertainly to reply, "Ain't nothing to be in on. I was fixing to ride out to your spread and tell you. I got that Indian agent, Dodsworth, to hire me. He's appointed me his point man for the drive. But there's nothing for you all to worry about. It really is an Indian agency drive, like he's been saying all along. Those sheep are bound for the Standing Rock, as a gift free and simple to the Navaho nation. There was never any big sheep outfit fixing to horn in on your range."

She stared up like a house cat stares at most mere humans for a long unwinking time. Then she decided, "If you're not out to double-cross us you are too stupid to be running around off a leash! Did you think we'd just wait and see, like bumps on a log? You're not the only one working for us on the sly. But I have to say you're about as big a fool as anyone ever hired. We *know* who owns that herd. The goddamn Irish-greaser Santa Fe ring is out to crush us Texas riders again and of *course* they've got pull with the damnyankee BIA. But that don't change the pure simple fact that Pedro Maxwell, the greasy sheep baron of the Pecos valley, is out to grab our cattle range!"

Chapter 12

Speaking as Latigo Shaw pretending to be Buck Crawford, Longarm doubted a Wyoming rider for the Cattlemen's Protective Association would have call to know many New Mexico sheep barons. So he replied, "Who are you talking about? I've et breakfast twice with Ed Dodsworth and met a couple of his hired sheepherders and three government men, so far. I ain't heard one make mention of anyone called Maxwell."

The tall imperious brunette called out, "Tell him about Pedro Maxwell, *segundo mio!*"

A hatchet-faced cuss all in black from his Boss Stetson down to his silver-spurred Justin boots stepped out of the shadowy arcade enclosing the paved patio to remark in the tone of a man who knew, "Maxwell likes you to call him Pete, even though his mother was a greaser and his sisters all look like gypsy dancers. The Maxwells and Chisums have divvied up the Pecos valley between 'em. Nobody grazes nothing but cows south of Fort Sumner to the Texas line and if they ain't branded with Chisum's long rail when they start out they soon will be. Uncle John has his own army of Tex-Mex riders tending more cows than you'd think you could fit in that much range, and they hold a hell of a lot of range by right of grit and gunpowder."

The *segundo* got out a smoke for himself as he went on, "Pedro Maxwell owns Fort Sumner and grazes everything north of the same down to the roots with his bucktoothed sheep. Has an army of his own, mounted or on foot, mostly Mex, so hardcased Anglos who don't herd sheep for him. They make sure nobody *else* grazes sheep on either side of the valley, all the way north to Las Vegas."

He lit his smoke and went on, "Sheep being sheep they multiply like rabbits and graze their world bald in no time. So Maxwell needs more range and knows better than to crowd Uncle John Chisum to his south. So he'd fixing to crowd *ussen*, figuring we ain't got the pull Uncle John has in Santa Fe. And figuring we ain't got the sand in our craws to stand up to him."

Judith glanced up at Longarm to demand, "Well?"

Longarm asked, mildly, "Who told you all about this devious plot?"

The *segundo* said, "Word gets around when an outfit's arming for a war. Fort Sumner being on the riverside Goodnight Trail, a lot of riders from all over break trail there to rest up a spell. So this Texas rider was at the bar in Bob Hargrove's saloon in Fort Sumner when some Mex riders were talking openly, albeit in Spanish, about hiring on with the Maxwells. Our pal never let on he savvied Spanish. He just listened sleepy-eyed as they plotted our ruination. Maxwell's lined up a mess of Basque sheepherders, harder than Mexicans when it comes to fighting on foot with rifles. They'll see to the sheep and drive off anybody who comes near 'em. Maxwell's hired just plain gunslicks, no offense, to ride his new range for him. Seems there's a lot of that breed left over around Fort Sumner since the shooting around Lincoln died away."

Longarm knew better than to tell the earnest-looking *segundo* he had to be full of shit. He said, "If what you say is true, I've been lied to and laughed at behind my back. I know Dodsworth ain't planning to move them merinos just

102

yet. He's waiting on more help he's sent for. He told me it would be coming from Washington."

Judith Morrison sniffed, "He no doubt meant Fort Sumner. But no matter. What do you aim to do about it, Latigo?"

Stalling for time to think, Longarm said, "Reckon I'd better pay more attention."

She demanded, "When are you fixing to start *shooting*? What are you waiting for, an egg in your beer? I thought we'd settled on a hundred dollars a sheepherder and five hundred for that Dodsworth cuss."

She let that sink in before she added, "We'll give you a thousand to finish off Pedro Maxwell himself."

Longarm said, "That sounds fair. Give me time to make certain. As I told you on the train, Miss Judy, I'm a professional. I have to be sure before I commence me an omelet. For once you bust an egg, there's no way to repair the damage and saloon talk is . . . well, saloon talk."

Her *segundo* growled, "I know the old boy from Bob Hargrove's saloon better than I know you, no offense."

Longarm lightly replied, "None taken. I still want to talk to gents I know better. Will you be here later this evening, Miss Judy?"

She said, "No. We mean to ride out during *La Siesta* when nobody's as likely to notice. I'll be out to the Rocking M if you have anything new to say, Latigo. I don't want to hear you say you have to check some more. I thought we had it established, aboard that train, that you were a man of *action*!"

Longarm said he was glad she recalled their . . . conversation aboard that night train and excused himself to go back to the hotel and spy some more.

After he'd left, Judith turned to her *segundo* to ask, "Well, what did you think of him, Angus?"

Angus Glourie, a man with a rep that made blood run cold down Texas way, shrugged dismissively to reply, "Not much. Talk is cheap. Anybody can say he's a big bad range detective. I haven't seen him *do* much."

Slats, who'd been standing a respectful distance near the archway, piped up to opine, "You ain't seen that old boy *slap leather*, Segundo! I startled him in a dark alley, earlier, and Judas Priest if he didn't have his six-gun in my face faster than most men blink their eyes!"

The *segundo* shrugged and pointed out, "You're still breathing, ain't you? Lots of old boys practice quick draws in front of a pier glass 'til they're good at it. Whipping out your gun is one thing. Whipping out your gun and *using* it's another."

Judith shrugged and said, "Two Ton Tobin says he's used his gun a time or two."

"Maybe he's just shy, then." The man who knew for certain *he* was a killer shrugged and added, "We'll know one way or the other, soon enough."

When Longarm got back to his hotel, his mind in a whirl, he found Dodsworth in a study off the lobby, writing a letter on hotel stationery. Longarm sat down beside him to produce his own field notebook and handed it over, saying, "Hang on to this for me. It's too hot for me to have on my person should lunatics with persecution manias get the drop on me."

As Dodsworth examined the notebook in wonder, Longarm said, "If anything happens to me, that one list of names may or many not be the ringleaders you're still up against. I may have been bullshitted by another crackpot."

As he leaned back in his own chair, looking bushed, Dodsworth demanded he explain. So Longarm tried to. When he got to the allegation they were all fronting for Pedro, or Pete, Maxwell, Dodsworth naturally wanted to know who in blue blazes Pete Maxwell might be.

Longarm wearily replied, "I'm sure his aim in life is to live in a fort by the side of the road and be a friend to man. But I fear he's a textbook example of a white-feathered crow."

Dodsworth blinked, "Come again?"

Longarm explained, "These college head shrinkers with a cage full of crows, a flocking species, took one crow out on the sly and painted just one of its feathers white. Then they put the crow back in the cage with its flock to see what might happen."

Dodsworth had been to college. He said, "I read about that experiment. It's been run more than once. The other crows either cower away or attack the one that's just a tad unusual in their eyes, right?"

Longarm nodded grimly and said, "Pete Maxwell was sent to college by a a rich dad and a refined mom. So his English is better than mine and his table manners tend to be more fancy. He inherited vast land holdings and a mess of sheep along with a whole army fort his dad bought off the war department. He converted the land into a ranch headquarters and rest stop on the Goodnight Loving trail. Thanks to his heritage, he's well connected in Santa Fe with the Irish Mex oligarchy that still runs New Mexico when Governor Wallace ain't looking. Thanks to his own brains, Pete stayed out of that big range war betwixt his kind and Uncle John Chisum's kind by steering clear of Lincoln Plaza, a hard two day's ride to his south and by treating riders from both sides the same when they dropped by to wet their whistles or lay low a spell. So he's naturally suspected of fucking stock and running the brands of his sisters. By now there's a whole lot of part-Mex or part-Indian gents here in the Southwest. But it's an article of faith that half-breeds can't be trusted."

He got out a couple of cheroots, handed one to Dodsworth, and lit 'em both up as he continued, "Even Mr. Mark Twain, as fair-minded a man as you'll catch writing books, made the half-breed Indian Joe an outcast and a killer in his book about Tom Sawyer. Pete Maxwell's three-quarters white, his mom being half-French and half-Mex, so you have to peer close to notice he ain't exactly Anglo-Saxon. But some do, and seeing a rich man make enemies without trying, old Pete's learned to fight back when he has to. The gunslicks on both sides in that Lincoln County war left Maxwell alone and treated Fort Sumner as neutral ground because the alternative was worse. Whether they admire his plumage or not, they knew he had the sand and the manpower to tip the scales either way."

He took a thoughtful drag on his cheroot and explained, "Doing business like an Anglo and running it like a Mex *patrón* gives what the Mexicans call a *comerciante* an edge you don't want to buck if it can be avoided. John Tunstall had such riders as Dick Brewer, Charlie Bowdre and Billy the Kid as part-time employees and pals. Pete Maxwell inherited whole *clans* of Mex *dependientes* sworn to back his every whim to the death. Some of them mean it. If a range war busts out betwixt them Texas cattle folk and the Maxwell outfit, you'll see blood on the moon."

Dodsworth pointed out, "But you said this Maxwell grazes his stock over on the Pecos and McKinley County is west of the Rio Grande. So how could trouble break out between them?"

Longarm said, "Some mean-hearted son of a bitch is out to stir such trouble up. He, she, or it has sold them proddy newcomers the notion that your BIA herd up the way is a ruse engineered by Pete Maxwell and his Santa Fe pals to wrest all that land they stole from the Navaho away from them. I got to figure out how to make them see the light. Just telling 'em the truth don't seem to work."

He got back to his feet, saying, "I'd best bring my home office up to speed on all this shit before siesta time. Which ain't far off, now. I'm commencing to feel like that sorcerer's apprentice who had all them fool brooms going every which way as he tried in vain to stop 'em."

Dodsworth said, "Before you go, I've another problem I could use some advice on."

Longarm told him to shoot. Dodsworth said, "It's Mac-Tavish. You heard him as much as call me a liar, earlier. He keeps changing his stories, plural. I've caught him contradicting himself more than once. The things he says about his past experiences fail to accord with his job application. When I pointed this out, he flustered that he'd had somebody fill out the forms for him because he doesn't know how to read and write. That other professional, DuVille, has tried to stay out of it. But I did get him to confide he has his doubts about MacTavish knowing which end of a sheep the shit may fall from."

Longarm soberly replied, "It ain't for me to say whether anyone ought to marry up with or fire another man. You're in charge out here. It's your call."

Dodsworth grimaced and said, "We're already so short-handed, and if it turned out I'd lost yet another herder for unjust cause . . ."

Longarm said, "I told you how my boss likes to sniff along the wires and across paper. Why don't we hand MacTavish to him? An immigrant from another country must have passed through places where they keep records of his travels."

Dodsworth brightened and asked, "You mean like immigration and naturalization at Castle Garden in New York?"

Longarm shrugged and said, "He might say he came in through Boston, or Canada, or just parted the seas and drove sheep across. Billy Vail will know better than me where to start."

Dodsworth left the matter in his hands and Longarm got back up to the telegraph office to send some wires. He held back on sending too many. Alerting Pete Maxwell and his pals in Santa Fe to the war talk before any war could bust out might be jumping the gun for a race that might still be avoided.

Longarm left Western Union with the sun glaring down from directly above and headed for La Posada Pilar to see if he still had as frisky a flop there. He figured he might get some answers to his telegrams by the time he felt more . . . rested.

Some of the shops he passed were already shuttered but

when he got to the taproom, which was serving more Anglos than Mexicans, he found things busy enough. Gluepants and Dallas were bellied up to the bar about where he'd last seen them. They spotted him and called him over to join them. As he gently elbowed his way through the crowd, he saw a trio of gents who reminded him of Pete Maxwell, hogging a table in a far corner. They were dressed like Anglo cattle buyers in suits and ties under high-crowned Stetson ten-gallons. *New* high-crowned Stetson ten-gallons. Only their *mestizo* features suggested they were the sort of gents you'd expect to observe *La Siesta* at this hour.

Hoping he was wrong, Longarm bellied up to the bar on the far side of Gluepants and Dallas with his back to the Mexican trio, keeping an eye on them in the back-bar mirror from under his lowered hat brim.

Sure enough, as Gluepants told a bawdy tale about a lonesome sheepherder, the three swarthy strangers rose from their table and commenced to spread out, all three of them staring at the back of Longarm's denim jacket as one moved along the front window, another slid along the back wall and the one in the middle just kept smiling sleepy as he drifted in.

So Gluepants was saying, "In the morning, as he counted his flock the old sheepherder says, 'One, two, three . . . good morning, darling . . . five, six . . . ' What the hey?"

For Longarm had spun away from the bar, shouting, "Hit the dirt!" in a loud tone of military command.

Then all hell broke loose.

Chapter 13

Less than two-thirds of the crowd, including the Mex near the back wall, dropped to the floor without thinking. But that thinned the field of fire enough for a good shot and, knowing the form of old, Longarm shot the one near the front first, to spin him out the open doorway as his own '73 Colt .45 landed just inside.

Such three-man teams always included a spokesman to hold your attention whilst the others flanked you. So the one in the middle was likely the spokesman and seeing he just stood there like a big-ass bird, Longarm put a round in his chest as he crabbed sideways and, sure enough, the one closer to the back wall rose on one knee to send a round through the cloud of gunsmoke Longarm had just left. That gunman caught Longarm's third shot with his face and left his spanking new Texas hat in midair as his shattered skull bounced off the plastered adobe behind him. Longarm crabbed farther, covering all concerned, but nobody else moved a muscle as they froze on their feet or bellies.

There came a long pregnant gunsmoke-scented pause and then Gluepants Gafferty croaked, from where he lay on the floor near the bar, "All right. If you didn't care for that one, let me tell you about the farmer's ugly daughter!"

So Longarm laughed, then most of them laughed and it

was Dallas who asked, getting to his feet, what the beef had been.

Longarm replied, loud enough for all to take it in, "Ain't certain, but if they weren't after me, they were after somebody at the bar just now. I was watching them in the backbar mirror. You can all judge the odds for yourselves. That six-gun by yonder doorway never drew herself."

A patron rising near the wall called out, "This one had an army .45 in his own hand when he lost his head a mite. Remind me never to draw on you when you're looking in the mirror, Buck!"

The general feeling he was one of them worked in Longarm's favor a few moments later when a brace of Albuquerque lawmen, one Anglo and the other Mex, came busting in with their own guns drawn.

By then Longarm had reloaded and reholstered and everyone but the three Mexicans he'd shot was up and about again. The Anglo lawman demanded to know why there was a dead man on the walk out front.

Longarm called back, "Two more in here. I was the one who shot the three of them. I had to because they were after me. I can't say why they were after me. I'd never seen them before."

Gluepants Gafferty said, "Put that Schofield away before it catches a chill on you, Curly. You know me and I seen it all. Buck Crawford, here, never said doodly shit to one of 'em and they ganged up on him three to one."

Curly moved in for a better look, whistled and decided, "They surely chose the wrong gringo to play *tu madre* with. You say they call you Buck and you do have some visible means of support, Mr. Crawford?"

Longarm nodded and said, "I work for the Bureau of Indian Affairs. I'm registered as Buck Crawford over at the Mountain View Hotel."

The Mex member of the two-man team said he'd heard there was a bunch of BIA agents over by the station and added he'd heard they'd been trying in vain to hire some of his own kids as sheepherders. Pointing at the one in the middle of the floor with his chin, the Mex said, "The three may have felt insulted, no?"

Curly hunkered down to roll that one over and pat him down for ID. He whistled when he opened a wallet to declare, "We got us a dead Mex lawman here! Seems he's a range detective working plainclothes for *Los Rurales*!"

The Mex lawman from north of the border smiled boyishly at Longarm and said, "You have permission to dance with my sister, Crawford. No man who guns a mother fucking *Rurale* can do wrong in *my* book!"

There came a general murmur of agreement, *Los Rurales* being one of the few subjects all men of good will agreed upon in those parts. The one called Curly told Longarm, "I hope you weren't planning on going anywheres for a spell, Mr. Crawford. It's just a formality, but the coroner might want you to come in and sign a deposition."

Longarm said his outfit was waiting on extra hands before they drove those sheep to Standing Rock. So they all had a drink to that and then the local lawmen sent a kid to fetch the county meat wagon.

During a lull in the conversation, Longarm got the barkeep, Pilar's uncle, aside to say he'd been wondering where she might be. The older Mexican looked through him as he gravely replied, "*El Señor* is mistaken. Is no woman of my family working here. We are people of respect. We do not know, nor do we wish for to know any people with *Los Rurales* after them, *comprende*?"

Longarm allowed he understood perfectly. He knew better than to ask if they had a flop for him upstairs now.

So *La Siesta* was in full flower and the sunny streets of Albuquerque were deserted as Longarm trudged on back to his hotel alone. You had to lie down *somewheres* when the sandstone walks were hot enough to bake tortillas on. He was feeling it serious by the time he made it to the thick walls of his hotel. The shade inside felt twenty degrees cooler and likely was.

As he crossed the lobby a she-male voice called his name. He peered into the gloom to spy two figures seated under a paper palm tree in a far corner. He had no idea why they grew paper palm trees in hotel lobbies. He went over to ask Marmion MacEwen and an expensively suited, balding cuss of around fifty what he could do for them.

The tall, tanned blonde had changed to a summer frock of printed cotton to perhaps draw fewer stares in town. She introduced her lobby companion as a Banker Forbes. When she told Banker Forbes to call him Buck Crawford Longarm knew she hadn't betrayed any confidances.

As Longarm sat down in a leather chair across from them, Marmion told him, "I bank with Mr. Forbes, here in town, as do most of my neighbors out along the Rio Puerco. He's naturally worried as we are about those hotheads who won't listen to reason."

Banker Forbes said, "I'm *twice* as worried as anyone else could get. I have a lot of loans outstanding over in McKinley County. A range war could put me out of business. You've no idea how hard it can be to get a man to repay a loan when he's dead, in jail or hiding out in the chaparral!"

"You loan out money without security?" Longarm marveled.

The banker sighed, "With beef prices rising we've competition from bigger Eastern banks. European investors are buying stock in pie-in-the-sky cattle kingdoms consisting of a dozen scrub cows and a water hole surrounded by open range nobody holds title to. I try to do better than that, but it isn't easy. Rancher with a proven quarter section along a water course finds it surprisingly easy to borrow against next year's beef sales in a rising market. I've got better than half our cash reserves tied up along the Rio Puerco and I shudder to think what will happen if half of them default on their loans!"

Longarm nodded soberly and said, "I follow your drift. French lawmen say you should search for romantic motives. I'd heard tell it makes more sense to figure who might make money on the deal. So let's imagine the worst that can happen. Let's imagine the BIA puts its head down and just drives six thousand sheep where they ain't welcome. Let's imagine an unwelcoming committee blazing away to stop them dead in their tracks with dead sheep, sheep dogs and sheepherders all over creation."

Forbes gasped, "Lew Wallace will declare martial law and those who don't hang will be running like blue blazes!"

Longarm answered, "I was about to say as much. So who stands to come out ahead?"

Marmion MacEwen said, "Certainly not the Navaho, the Bureau of Indian Affairs or those of us with common sense! That Lincoln County mess left ranchers who tried to stay out of it tarred with the same brush. Even as we speak surviving gunslicks prey on the herds still left for lack of any other income. As the blood money dried up hired guns like Jesse Evans, Charlie Bowdre, Tom O'Folliard and that wild Billy Bonney went into business for themselves, raiding stock off everybody! I fear things may get even worse over on the Rio Puerco, where the country is even wilder. We have to nip it in the bud, Buck!"

Longarm shrugged and said, "Well, the simple truth about them sheep seems to fall on deaf ears. Or ears as don't want to hear. Going by past history, most of the shooting on both sides comes from the guns of the least sensible riders on either side. The war lords egging them on don't seem to get shot as often. If we could figure out who'd been stirring up dust to blind the bulls, we might be able to make 'em stop, in time."

They were joined by Reporter Phalen from the *Santa Fe Weekly Democrat*. He flopped in another chair with an expression of sheer admiration to declare, "I've been looking all over for you! They told me at La Posada Pilar what you'd done. Our city desk in Santa Fe is burning up the wires, trying to find out more about those *Rurale* deserters."

As Marmion asked what they were talking about, Longarm said he hadn't heard those poor unfortunates had deserted anything.

Phalen said, "Their captain, down at the border crossing, says they were never sent up this way after anybody and suggests they were acting on their own as paid assassins. He said there are no Mexican wants on anybody called Buck Crawford."

When Marmion repeated her question, the reporter told her and made it sound so exciting Longarm wished he'd been there to see it.

The willowy blonde stared thunderghasted at Longarm and gasped, "You never said a word about a gunfight when you came in, just now!"

To which Longarm could only reply, truthfully, "I didn't see as it had anything to do with things over in McKinley County, ma'am."

She sobbed, "Someone's out to kill you before you can expose them as the troublemakers they have to be! Can't you see that?"

Banker Forbes looked fit to upchuck as he chimed in, "This game is getting too rich for my blood by half! Sending out for hired guns from south of the border is just plain mad dog lunacy and who in God's name could have *considered* such a crazy move?"

"Mad dog, most likely," said Longarm, not caring to go into his own suspicion that those *Rurales* had been innocent of any connection with the mastermind behind his other woes.

Banker Forbes got to his feet, allowing he had to go consult with his business partners about these new developements. Longarm got up, telling Reporter Phalen he aimed to take a flop upstairs and that, no offense, Reporter Phalen was not his type.

The reporter laughed and said he had to get back to the Western Union to file another flash.

Longarm never invited Marmion MacEwen. She just

seemed to be going up the stairs with him. She'd said she was staying there at the Mountain View.

It was even cooler upstairs, where shade and random drafts worked together. As they moved along the dimly lit hallway Marmion said she'd be staying in town until the trouble blew over. She said, "I'm terrible frightened, Deputy Long. A woman alone can be so tempting to a certain kind when the law flies out the window and I don't know who my friends or enemies are of late. There's been so much bitter talk, with wild accusations fluttering about like bats in the darker parts of people's minds. How much longer do we have to wait for things to come to a head?"

He said, "Not long, now. Agent Dodsworth's inclined to dither. But his dithering time is running out as the Indians fidget at Standing Rock. He has to fish or cut bait. If those extra herders he's sent for don't get here soon we're going to have to start without them and I hope you never told Banker Forbes who I really was'."

She said, "Of course not. You asked me not to. How can you possibly hope to drive six thousand sheep over a hundred miles with the help you have on hand, Deputy Long?"

He said, "Call me Buck, for now. Saves making slips when you stick to one alias at a time. We can't drive six thousand sheep *ten* miles with the manpower on hand. Somebody, likely the same somebody who has your Texas pals all het up, has put out the word that no local stockmen who enjoy life ought to help us out with that herd. Meanwhile I've been out to convince old Dodsworth there's more than one way to skin a cat and a while earlier, today, he showed more willingness to learn than I'd hoped for and I've been considering the advantages of not being set in your ways when they give you a hard row to hoe. This here's my room, Miss Marmion. Where might you be staying up here?"

She lowered her lashes and said, "I don't want to be alone up here. I'm so afraid. So very very afraid, and last night, when I felt your strong arms around me . . . Oh, Buck, what are we doing out here in the hall in this ridiculous verticle position?"

That was a good question. It was nigh dark in his room despite the hour because the windows were shuttered against the blaze outside. He shut and barred the door after them. As he turned from doing so she was on her toes, flattened against the front of him with her arms around his neck and her face tilted up to him in welcome. So he kissed her and it felt like coming home to the girl of his dreams after fighting a war or discovering another continent. So he swept her up to carry her on to the bed and they didn't have to say a word as they just went to bed like they'd always done before he'd gone away. But after he'd stripped her bare and mounted her like a natural man, it still sent electric shocks down his spine to discover it just wasn't true that all cats were gray in the dark.

As he sank it to the roots to just shudder inside her, hardly daring to move his hips as she languidly wrapped her long legs around him, she softly gasped, "What's happening to us? How are you doing that? I was only expecting you to fuck me, darling!"

He murmured, "I'd have been satisfied with that, too. I'm sorry. I just can't help it. I'm fixing to come!"

So he did, feeling it down to his curled toes as she bit down with her moist innards to milk his old organ grinder as it shot its wad in her. And then he was moving his hips like a schoolboy in a whorehouse as he just had to shoot his wad again in anything that grand!

Marmion was moaning, "Yes, yes, yesss!" as she took all he had to give and gave it back with her tight horsewoman's hips thrusting in perfect time as if they'd danced this dance together since they got thrown out of the Garden of Eden until, as all things must, it ended with the two of them gasping for breath at the bottom of their sea of love.

It took a spell, with him just holding her against him as they fought for breath. When Marmion was able to talk

116

again she asked him what was so funny. He patted her beautiful bare butt and assured her, "I wasn't laughing at you, little darling. I was laughing at how the best-laid plans of mice and men gang aft agley, like you Scotch folk say."

She answered, "Oh, were you planning on doing this with somebody else this afternoon?"

He didn't think she'd cotton to a truthful answer. So he kissed the part in her hair and said, "There ain't nobody else, in all the world, this afternoon."

Chapter 14

As the widow of a happy marriage who said she'd just discovered sex for the first time, Marmion wanted to tag along when Longarm said he had to go back to the telegraph office after four. He warned her, "You might not be safe on the streets with me right now, little darling. We can't be certain there were only three mean Mexicans after me and until we find out, you'll be safer undercover when you're in my company. If you don't feel right here in this hotel, might you have any friends in town you can hole up with?"

She said, "I could stay with Banker Forbes and his family. But we'd find it awkward at bedtime. I guess I'll just wait here whilst you go on about your business in town, you meanie."

They sealed the bargain dog-style and he got dressed to break cover, like it or not. At the Western Union he found a wire from Billy Vail confirming a red-bearded Scotchman giving his name as Hamish McTavish and giving his profession as sheepherding had disembarked in Alexandria, Virginia, handy to Washington D.C. the previous October. Old Billy, bless him, said he'd sent a transatlantic cable to a Scotch office as kept records of such things. Billy said you weren't allowed to wear the tartan of another clan nor call yourself a qualified shepherd in Scotland unless you

119

could prove it. There were things to be said about picky, picky pencil-pushing when you didn't have to do it your ownself.

He sent some wires of his own and as he paid for them the telegraph clerk shoved a quarter back across the counter at him, asking, "Can't you do better than this Canadian quarter?"

Longarm felt no call to argue silver was silver. He fished out another coin, saying, "My mistake. Must have been given it in change here at my hotel."

Outside he flicked the Canadian coin away. Longarm started to walk on, then to light up. Looking around, he noticed that Mex kid hunkered in the same spot under that same hat. He realized the dumb little shit had doubled back for his proud possession.

Dumb kids were tough to question. They tended to think they were too tough for you when you refrained from hurting them seriously.

Longarm considered, then stepped outside, pretending not to notice the punk on his tail as he ambled northwest into the older part of town.

He crossed the plaza as it was coming back to life, with the evening *paseo* of flirty gals strolling round it one way whilst duded-up young studs strutted the other.

He circled some as if looking to get laid and then he ducked into a doorway marked POLICIA COMISARIA. The unifomed Mex at the desk asked in English what Longarm wanted.

Longarm smiled indulgently and said, "I feel sort of dumb, bothering you with such petty shit, Sergeant. But I don't want to smack a kid and this fresh young squirt just picked my pocket. Bumped into me like it was an accident. I thought it was until I counted my change."

The local lawman looked pained and replied, "You say this *muchacho* got some *small change* off you?"

Longarm nodded and said, "I know I'd never prove it, as a rule, but the kid got my lucky coin and I'd really like it back."

120

"Lucky coin?" the copper badge asked thoughtfully.

Longarm said, "Canadian quarter dollar. Image of Queen Victoria at a younger age stamped on it."

The police sergeant called a lesser light from the ward room and curtly ordered him in Spanish to see if the fucking gringo knew what he was talking about.

The two of them went outside. The kid and his hat were under a street lamp to their right, trying to look innocent. When he spotted them there he looked as if he was fixing to run. The Mex copper badge called out, "Don't be stupid, Pablo Vargas! I know where you live. I know your people. Get your skinny ass over here, *muchacho!*"

The kid came over, sullenly, protesting, "I have done nothing. Do not believe that *maricon*. He was trying for to queer me, earlier!"

The uniformed Mex frog-marched the kid inside and they made him empty his pockets out on the desk. He'd had seventy-eight cents in change on him. One of the quarters bore the profile of Queen Victoria.

When the desk sergeant asked for an explanation, the kid truthfully replied, "I found it. On the walk. Over by the telegraph office. When has it become a crime for to carry a Canadian coin for luck?"

The sergeant beamed as he replied, "When you take it from the pocket of another. I have warned you before we had our eyes on you, *muchacho!*"

The sergeant told Longarm, "Has no father. Runs errands for his *bruja* of a grandmother who deals in love charms."

The sergeant waited until they'd locked the kid up in the back before he confided to Longarm, "We can't ask the night court to try him on such a charge, señor. How much time can they give him for stealing a worthless coin? May I make a suggestion?"

Longarm said he'd go along with anything the town law thought best, knowing what they were going to suggest. So half an hour later, after Longarm had enjoyed a few smokes in the doorway, watching the *paseo* as the shadows lengthened, an older woman wearing a black shawl over her head came up the walk to stop dead in her tracks and blanch when she saw *El Brazo Largo* standing there, regarding her with a knowing smile.

Longarm ticked his hat brim to her, out of earshot of the lawmen inside, as he murmured, "*Buenoches*, Señora Vargas. I have agreed to release your grandson into your custody. But first I would like a private word with you about . . . Mexican politics."

She stammered she didn't understand. He just kept smiling as he said, "*El Telegrafo* is a marvelous invention. It allows you to reach your own friends south of the border, it allows *me* to reach *my* friends south of the border and I wonder what they would think of a woman of the people who sucks up to *Los Rurales*. What do *you* think they would consider just treatment for such a . . . person, señora?"

"I do not know what *El Señor* is talking about!" she sobbed.

He said, "I wish it known I have just left town by rail. Once this is known south of the border I mean nothing but the greatest respect for *La Señora* Vargas."

He let that sink in before he added, "None of my friends south of the border need ever hear the name of *La Señora* Vargas, as long as my friends *north* of the border feel there is no need to send a *telegramo* I am going to leave in a safe place. That is all you need to understand and I feel sure you will because you strike me as a woman of great common sense."

The crone fluttered her lashes as if she found him most gallant and they went inside to get her somewhat abashed grandson out. She made him thank *El Señor* for refusing to press charges.

By now the sun was setting and *El Paseo* was heating up. As he stood there thoughtfully smoking, more than one passing señorita fluttered her lashes and quickly looked away. That was the way life worked. When a man had nothing waiting for him at home nobody wanted to flutter her lashes at him. When he was lined up for the night, other women circled him like sharks scenting blood in the water.

He walked back to the hotel, muttering to himself, and took Marmion out to supper at a real French restaurant, seeing it seemed safe to appear in public with her now. He couldn't tell her what he'd done to change the odds. When she asked, he said he was packing a lucky coin.

They wound up in the tap room, back at their hotel, since it was a tad early to get back in bed together. BIA Agent Tanner was there, along with Hoffmann from Agriculture. They said Dodsworth was up in his room, feeling poorly after eating oysters, earlier, in the hotel dining room.

Tanner said he'd told his boss not to trust oysters shipped all the way in from California on ice, this late in the season.

Hoffmann said he'd had half a dozen oysters for supper, raw, and felt just fine.

Tanner suggested he wait a bit. Then he added, hopefully, "Of course, Dodsworth might be coming down with a mortified appendix, like Brigham Young died from, back in '77."

Longarm asked, "What did the doctor say?"

Tanner said, "He won't let us send for a doctor. He's afraid they'll put him in the hospital and *then* where will he be?"

"Alive, for openers," Longarm muttered. He turned to Marmion to tell her, "I'd better go up and have a look at him. I'm no doc, but I've met up with food poisoning before."

She said she had some nursing experience at a Texas clinic in her misspent youth. So he let her tag along.

He knocked discreetly and went in first to find Dodsworth in his nightshirt atop the covers, soaked in sweat. Longarm moved in to feel his brow and say, "You're buring up, old son. This don't look good. You'd better let us fetch you a doctor."

Dodsworth said, "I don't want a doctor. I know what it

123

is. I've had these spells before. It's recurrent malaria. If you let the sawbones at me they'll put me in the hospital and try to ship me home."

"Maybe that's where you belong," Longarm said, soberly.

Dodsworth swore and insisted, "Nonesense! By the time I was halfway there this fever would break and leave me with egg on my face and all those sheep going nowhere!"

Longarm said, "I've a lady in the hall with nursing experience, I want her to take a look at you."

Dodsworth was muttering to himself as Longarm let Marmion in. She showed them both how come she managed her own cattle spread when she paid no mind to his protests but had Longarm wet and wring out a hotel towel at the corner washstand whilst she took Dodsworth's pulse.

As she took the damp towel and placed it on the sick man's fevered brow she said, "Malaria. Bad air. You see a lot of it in Texas near the Gulf coast swamps. You catch it breaking fumes that rise at night from rotting vegetation. Once you've caught it, the chills and fever come and go with minds of their own. This poor man needs quinine. Now."

Dodsworth waved a limp hand at the hotel tumbler and pill boxes on his bed table to croak, "I've taken enough to where my ears are ringing. I'll be all right by this time tomorrow. You're right, ma'am. It comes and it goes. When it comes I can barely think straight. When it goes I'm right as rain and it feels as if I'll never come down with it again. So just let me be. I'll get better. I have to get better. Those Indians are waiting for us at Standing Rock and I can't fail them. How are they to take delivery of all that stock if I can't make it?"

Longarm said, "You could delegate authority. Lord Nelson never wanted to. But when he had to, his fleet still won at Trafalgar, you know."

Dodsworth croaked, "Kiss me, Hardy, I'm dying!" and

commenced to laugh like hell. They had to laugh, too, and you had to admire the sand in his craw, even if he was pushing determination to stupidity.

Marmion told Longarm, "There's nothing we can do for him now but allow nature to take its course. You shouldn't take more quinine once your ears start ringing. The fever will break of its own accord if it . . . means to. Why don't we let him see if he can sleep? He needs to lie very, very quiet and our presence may be disturbing him."

As she rose to tiptoe out, Longarm followed, but out in the hall he asked her, "Are you sure? It don't seem right, leaving him alone in there like that."

She said, "He's going to die or get better, whether somebody holds his hand or not. I'm pretty sure he'll get better. That sweating is a good sign. I've never heard of anyone dying soaked in sweat. It's when they go dry with their temperature so high that you have to brace yourself for the end."

Longarm decided, "I'm fixing to tell the night clerk to keep an eye on him and call me if he goes dry then. You want to stay up here and wait whilst I go down to the lobby?"

She archly threatened to start without him if he didn't get back soon to do right by her. They kissed in the hall near his door and she went in to wait for him. He went down the stairs grinning. He was jawing with the night clerk at the desk when Reporter Phalen of the *Santa Fe Weekly Democrat* came in from the street.

Phalen said, "I'm glad you're still up and about. I just got a wire from our press room up in Santa Fe. It appears there's trouble brewing over in McKinley County!"

Longarm replied, "I don't see how it can. We're still waiting on them four professional sheepherders and now Dodsworth's down with the ague. Do they get here tonight, and they won't, we'd never move them sheep a country mile 'til he gets better or turns the chore over to somebody else."

The reporter said, "I'm not talking about that. I'm talking about the far bigger Maxwell herd."

Longarm snorted, "There ain't no Maxwell herd. No Maxwell herd headed for Standing Rock, least ways. Some troublemaker's been spreading shit about a legitimate government operation being a front engineered by the Santa Fe Ring to replace all them Texas cows with New Mexican sheep. It ain't so. Pure imagination has stirred up a bunch of hotheads with shit house rumors."

The local reporter demanded, "If there's nothing to it, how come Pete Maxwell's been signing on extra help over in Fort Sumner? If there's nothing to it, how come Pete Maxwell's signed on notorious gunfighters to back the play of his Mex vaqueros and *pastores*?"

Longarm demanded, "Who says he has?"

The reporter replied, "Pete Maxwell, on paper. Posted on the wall of Hargrove's Saloon. Five hundred a month and found for experienced gunmen with bonus money paid for saddles emptied in the course of his big push from the Pecos clean across the Continental Divide!"

Longarm scowled and asked, "You've *seen* such an offer in writing?"

The reporter said, "Not yet. My city editor has. Seems some riders passing through Fort Sumner helped themselves to the posters and carried them far as Santa Fe. By now some have probably made it as far west as McKinley County. My paper wants me to find out whether those cattle men are likely to wait for the sheepherders or ride east to meet them!"

Longarm swore and said, "I'd better see what's really going on!"

Chapter 15

Marmion was a good sport about it when he told her he had to go out again. It was barely bedtime for their own kind, so the old town was up and at 'em, with most of the gals at the *paseo* around the plaza still holding out for the man of their dreams.

Longarm scouted up that night court they'd mentioned at the police station and found it mostly dealt with fighting drunks. He spoke to the bailiff and, during a lull, the Mexican judge invited Longarm back to his chambers for that private word the gringo wanted, whoever in thunder he was.

Longarm produced his badge and federal warrant, leveling with the robed and flattered minor official as he explained his needs.

His Honor allowed a lawman working undercover was better off not packing court orders under his true identity. He said he'd have a discreet word in the morning with his presiding superior, the district attorney and their coroner, leaving "Buck Crawford" free to depart from the city limits of Albuquerque. So Longarm went back to the hotel to make it up to Marmion.

The magic was still there, but as some of the desperation for more subsided to sheer contentment, they got some sleep, waking up now and then in each other's arms until, by morning, they were starved for food as well.

They got cleaned up and dressed, dropping in on Dodsworth first to discover him sound asleep with his fever broken. Marmion checked his pulse as Longarm covered him with a sheet lest he catch a chill. She said his heartbeat was strong and slowed down to normal. So they went upstairs to have breakfast. They found the less know-it-all BIA agent, Roberts, sharing a table with that French Canadian sheepherder, DuVille. When they asked he told them it looked as if Dodsworth had been right about his own malaria.

Longarm said, "He won't be up to riding nowhere for a day or so, even if them other sheepherders show up."

Roberts said, "They won't. They just wired from Chicago. Seems they took the wrong train west and had to double back. They said they'd wire progress reports from Omaha, Cheyenne and Denver. Asking directions out your way can inspire weird western humor. I fail to see what was so funny about putting our extra hands on a train to New Orleans."

Longarm smiled thinly and observed, "They call it rawhiding. I agree it ain't funny. In the meantime, seeing the rest of you can't possibly move out for a few days, I thought I'd grab a stagecoach over to Fort Sumner and have a word with Pete Maxwell in the flesh. The rumors about him and us working in cahoots ain't true. But he might be able to put us on to how the rumor started."

Marmion said, "If you're going over to the Pecos, I'm going with you."

She sounded as if she meant it and seemed braced for an argument.

But Longarm nodded and said, "Of course you are, Miss Marmion. I want somebody raising cows along the Rio Puerco to hear it from the horse's mouth and mayhaps set her neighbors straight."

It wouldn't have been discreet to add he wanted to keep

an eye on her and had nobody lined up at what promised to be an overnight visit.

Marmion was like a kid promised a trip to the circus as she changed back into her riding outfit, holstered Schofield and all. He left Dancer in the hotel stable and walked her the short way to the stagecoach depot. He didn't have to tell an experienced rider why they were boarding a stage-coach for the grueling eighteen-hour ride, involving a change at Santa Rosa. It would have taken them three or four days on the trail had they elected to ride their own broncs.

The stage lines that still crossed much of the thinly set-tled southwest were commencing to feel slow to folk spoiled by the iron horse, which got you there four to six times sooner. But it was still a hell of an improvement on just plain riding.

The notion of hauling mail and passengers in stages, changing to fresh teams every twelve to fifteen miles, had been invented back in the old countries and had never been improved upon until Mr. Watt perfected the steam engine. In spite of foolish books like *Black Beauty*, horses were not windup toys you could stop and start like steam engines. A horse or better yet a Spanish saddle mule, in dry country, could go all out for around a mile, or trot at nine miles an hour for a couple of hours. After which it was bushed for the day and needed to rest up for the rest of the same. Hence, whilst a cavalry column on good stock might aver-age thirty miles a day, walking the horses, trotting them and resting them along the way, a stagecoach could roll a hundred miles in twelve hours, allowing for stops along the way to change teams and allow passengers to stretch their legs and crap on occasion.

Santa Rosa on the Pecos was that far from Albuquerque on the Rio Grande. A few hours longer when you added in the twists in the trail. So leaving Albuquerque around nine in the morning would put them in Santa Rosa around ten or eleven at night. At Santa Rosa you caught a northsouth stagecoach following the Goodnight Trail down to West Texas by way of Fort Sumner, Roswell and such. When she suggested they might lay over for the night in Santa Rosa, Longarm explained it would depend on their connections. Folk moved cross country by stagecoach to get there, not for comfort. Fort Sumner lay three or four hours down the Pecos from Santa Rosa and served the trail-weary traveler around the clock.

Marmion allowed he knew more than she did about such matters. Marmion was one of those gals who seemed easy to get along with in spite of the way they so often got their way.

They found their east-bound Concord coach uncrowded, with just a Mex gal and an Anglo couple sharing the twelve seats inside. They rolled out of town closer to nine-thirty. By the time they stopped to change teams around eleven, they all knew one another by first names. The Anglo new-lyweds were Jim and Nancy. The Mex gal said she was called Felicidad and didn't have as much to say.

From there on the trip got even less interesting. The country rose between the south-flowing rivers to the east and west as a less dramatic extention of the Front Range, the Sangre de Cristos, Capitan, Guadalupes and so on. Trails across from river to river naturally went where the land lay lowest. The stage line had built their relay stops near water wherever possible. So they followed Cedar Creek a spell and enjoyed a longer twenty-minute dinner stop at plank tables shaded by piñon pines before they had to move on across a rolling stretch of high chaparral and more patches of piñon, juniper and such. Folk in those parts called the same tree cedar or juniper, depending on where they were from, and, in either case, it looked like it ought to be growing on either side of a cemetery gate.

They made better time on the long downgrade along Posada Creek. But they'd just changed mules when they were jumped by would-be road agents.

They looked to be Mex or mayhaps Mescalero

teenagers, whooping in from either side, pegging wild pistol shots as they demanded the coach *no me jodas,* stop, and throw down the strong box. But the jehu whipped the mules into a dead run with his ribbons whilst the shotgun messenger held them at a respectful distance with his repeating Henry.

Longarm tried his luck out his side whilst Marmion blazed away with her Schofield and at one point yelled, "I got one!"

Felicidad sat frozen in her seat, mumbling to her rosary beads. Nancy was screaming fit to bust whilst Jim lay in a fetal position on the floor betwixt the seats. And then it was over, with the coach tearing down the trail lickety-split and the would-be road agents reined in to shout dreadful things about their mothers.

The sun was setting as they stopped for a hasty supper closer to the Pecos. Nobody could see the expression on Nancy's face as her groom explained yet again how he'd suffered this nervous condition since some blasting powder had gone off, premature, and made an awful mess of his favorite uncle. Longarm was too kind-hearted to tell the fool to just shut up and let nature take its course. His new bride was either going to let it go or she was never going to let him live it down. Nothing Jim could do or say could change that. Nancy seemed like a good kid, but Longarm suspected Jim's nervous condition might come up way on down the pike whenever they had an argument, if they stayed together that long. That old saw about a coward dying a thousand deaths had been written down with events like that afternoon's in mind.

Marmion seemed sort of proud of the way *her* escort had held up under fire. But, like Longarm, she pretended to buy Jim's tale of woe. She allowed how, down to that Texas clinic, they'd had cases of big strong men who fainted when they had a boil lanced. She's heard Napoleon was terrified of house cats and nobody had ever said *he* was a sissy.

They enjoyed a longer meal break than usual because the stagecoach crew had to write up a report on the attempted robbery. They asked the passengers to look it over and initial it. Longarm said he doubted they'd had a close call with Billy the Kid's notorious gang, but allowed they had the bare plot about right. The stage line would notify the sheriff's department and they'd likely send somebody out to see if Marmion really dropped one of them. They took down her home address and said she might hear more from them if she'd hit anybody with a bounty posted on his hide.

They rolled into Santa Rosa, north of the swamps where Posada Creek met the Pecos, later than usual to find the southbound night coach waiting on them, or waiting on the mail bags, that was, with its own passengers fit to be tied.

Marmion asked Longarm why they couldn't overnight in Santa Rosa and catch another stagecoach in the morning. He ruefully explained things didn't work that way. He said, "You make connections where there's connections to be made. There ain't no morning stagecoach. The southbound leaves the railroad town of Las Vegas according to when trains stop there to drop off mail. Won't be another coach through here until tomorrow afternoon."

She asked what there was to do around Santa Rosa whilst they waited. He explained there was little more than a stage stop in the middle of nowheres much and she settled for dozing against his shoulder in the more crowded night coach south.

They rolled into Fort Sumner in the wee small hours, or, least ways, the night coach slowed down to drop just the two of them off there.

Fort Sumner was neither a town nor what many pictured when they heard the word *fort*. The Indian fighting army had no call to erect walls around a garrison of regimental strength. An outpost manned by a troop or company might feel safer with a watchtower behind a stockade. But Mister Lo seldom rode in war bands numbering more than thirty, if that many, so a six-hundred man regiment posted a perimeter guard after dark and trusted Mister Lo's instincts for self-preservation.

Fort Sumner had been built with local labor and materials under the supervision of army engineers in the '60s, mostly with the Navaho agency at nearby Bosque Redondo in mind. So the ring of adobe buildings around a central parade ground had become redundant when the Navaho were allowed to return to the Four Corners and the newer Fort Stanton had been built a couple of days south to ride herd on the Mescalero and guard another eastwest route betwixt the Pecos and Rio Grande flood plains.

The action and financial rewards down that way had inspired the recently ended Lincoln County War, but Fort Sumner sat it out in the shade.

Pete Maxwell's father, Lucien, had bought the fort lock, stock and barrel from the war department and moved his family and grazing operations to Fort Sumner in the early '70s, to be buried in the fort's military cemetery. He left the whole shebang to Pete, who ran it as his company headquarters and profitable trail town, residing in the former commanding officer's house with his closer kin and important dependents sharing officer's row.

More interested in his vast herds than the trail town sidelines, he'd delegated authority and appointed one Alejandro Segura as *alcalde* over the mostly Mex permanent residents. Suitable army facilities were leased around what was now the plaza to be run as saloons, stables, a general store, road houses and, over in the old army hospital, a residence of ill repute for whores or outlaw's *mujeres*, depending on who you asked.

Over the years since the army had left, the fort had slopped over around the edges, with Mex adobes thrown up helter-skelter, punctuated by a cemetery and a peach orchard, planted by Navaho prisoners, which was beginning to bear tolerable crops of fruit.

Fort Sumner could be taken at first glance for just another southwestern town by newcomers, until they tried to do business without the approval of the right people. It was understood that Fort Sumner was a live-and-let-live little town, as long as you let others live. There were stories of bad men barging in to declare themselves the bees' knees, but somehow they always managed to get shot by a person or persons unknown before the night was out.

Longarm checked them into the former bachelor officer's quarters, now run as a spartan roadhouse with compact but clean separate rooms, before he told Marmion he had to drop by Hargrove's Saloon before he got in bed with her.

Marmion protested, "It's way after midninght, darling. It's time all the good little boys and girls were in bed!"

He said, "I know. I aim to see if there are any *bad* little boys and girls still up and about at this hour."

Chapter 16

Hargrove's Saloon was set up in the former officer's club and hence looked more like a saloon than some with its mahogany bar and matching tables. A mixed bag of Anglo and Mex riders were playing five card stud in a corner. No body was at the bar as Longarm moseyed over, hooked a boot on the brass rail and allowed he'd have a shot of their famous Forty Rod with a beer chaser.

The night manager, an Irish-Mex brew they called Paddy Herrerra, was friendly but firm as he said, while pouring, "I know why you're here, Uncle Sam. None of them federal wants have been by the last six months. I understand Dave Rudabaugh's been seen recent over in the Texas Panhandle to the east. Some say the Kid's working as a saloon swamper down in Shakespeare since he gunned Joe Grant, if he gunned Joe Grant. I was off that night."

Longarm swallowed the shot of Forty Rod to show he was a man, sent some suds after it to ease the pain and said, "I'm not here to arrest nobody, I hope. Those innocent lambs who frequent these parts between cattle raids are matters for the federal marshal in Santa Fe and he must not give a shit. My business here is with your patron, Don Pedro of the neighborly ways."

Paddy looked sincere as he shook his head and said,

"You got to understand how it is, Uncle Sam. Them unemployed guns left over from both the shot up sides have to make money some damn way. So they made peace with one another and went into the cattle business for themselves."

Longarm sipped more suds and said, "I understand the going price for an uncertainly branded cow stands around ten dollars a head, right?"

Paddy shrugged and replied, "Do I look like a beef buyer? As to old Pete, over to the big house, he raises sheep and, so far, none of the boys of whom we speak have stole a single lamb. He's spread the word it's no skin off his nose how others get by in this cruel world as long as they don't mix with any of his *partidos* or *pastores* out on the range and they treat all persons and property here in his private town civilized. So mayhaps some of the boys drop by from time to time, but when in town they behave themselves, spend money and treat the *putas* with respect."

He took Longarm's beer stein to top it with more suds as he chuckled fondly and said, *"Mierda!* Doc Scurlock and Charlie Bowdre have even *married up* with a couple of home town *muchachas."*

Longarm said, "I dunno, Paddy. Heard-tell the Kid shot Joe Grant at this very bar."

The night manager easily replied, "I wasn't here and Joe Grant rode in from other parts, making war talk about regulars who *belonged* here. I ain't saying it never happened, mind, but if it did, the stranger had it coming. I've served Billy the Kid and Chisum riders at the same time at this very bar and the Kid is said to hate Uncle John Chisum like fire."

As Longarm sipped more suds the authority on matters along the Pecos explained, "Kid's never forgiven the Chisums for not sending help when things came to a head in Lincoln Plaza and he says Uncle John owes him and his pals back pay for the last weeks of that war."

Longarm said, "Paddy, I ain't here to discuss the past. It's the *future* I'm concerned with. What can you tell me about a HELP WANTED notice, said to have been posted within these very walls, offering handsome wages for riders willing to fight in another range war entire?"

The night manager looked confounded and replied, "In here? Inviting gun hands to sign on for trouble? For who? Against whom?"

Longarm repeated what Reporter Phalen had told him in Albuquerque. The Irish-Mex shook his head to reply, "Never happened. I'd have noticed. Old Pete never hires Anglos *direct* for *any* task. I work here for Bob Hargrove who rents this property from Pete. The same applied to most everybody you might find employed here in town, Anglo or Mex. Pete's way bigger sheep operation is run on the Mex *partidario* system, too complicated for you or other Anglo riders to grasp. You boys hire on with an outfit for a set salary, to be given a raise or fired as things may transpire. That ain't the way the business is done in Spanish. A *comerciante grande* such as Don Pedro grubstakes *partidos* or middlemen, and they in turn put together and manage stretches of range with their majordomos, *caporals* and such, who are most often kin or in-laws. The vaqueros or *pastores* in the field ain't on fixed wages. Their needs are seen to by their *partidos*, acting through their *caporales* with advice from his majordomo, so . . ."

"You're right, it's too complicated for this child," Longarm cut in, adding, "Are you telling me in essence that Pete Maxwell ain't hiring Anglo riders, in any capacity?"

"That's about the size of it," Paddy replied, leaning forward to confide, "Now that he's a deputy sheriff with higher aspirations, that long drink of water, Pat Garrett, tells folk down to Lincoln County he used to ride for Pete Maxwell as a top hand. But he worked behind this bar with me for Bob Hargrove after going bust as a buffalo hunter. I ain't ashamed of what I do for an honest living. But now that he's on the county that tall drink of water's too proud to admit to what he really did up this way."

He reached for Longarm's beer stein, saying, "Don Pedro don't hire Anglo riders. He knows what they say about him behind his back and he's better with Mex help."

Longarm covered the stein with his hand and said, "I've had enough, thanks. Got to get some shut-eye after a mighty tedious day. What do I owe you, Paddy?"

The Irish-Mex said, "On the house. I've orders to be friendly with both sides."

Longarm pressed a cheroot on him and left, feeling the beer, or more likely the Forty Rod a mite. They called such trade whisky Forty Rod because it took a real man to walk forty rods without falling down after he'd put away more than one.

Back in their hired cubby hole Longarm found Marmion asleep after her own miserable day aboard a jolting stagecoach. When he shucked his duds and got under the covers with her she woke up, a lot, for she was naked as a jay after her first forty winks.

But, thanks to the rough day they'd had, it didn't take as much slap and tickle to calm her nerves and as they cuddled, afterwards, snug and half asleep, she asked if he'd found out anything.

He said, "I want to hear it from Don Pedro, himself, but it sure looks like somebody closer to the Rio Grande has been lying like a rug just to stir up trouble. As I told you long before we got here, Pete Maxwell is shrewd as they come. Avoided and still avoids taking sides, tries to stay in good with everybody, and prefers to have Mex help."

Being from Texas, Marmion decided Maxwell sounded like a *greaser* who knew his place.

Longarm said, "His place is the north end of the Pecos valley. I said he was smart, not yellow. Just scraping and bowing wouldn't hold the wolves at bay in these parts. These parts are still poorly policed and infested with hard-eyed men, Anglo, Mex and Mescalero. Don Pedro lives and lets live by judicious use of the carrot and the stick. He'd have it known he's a good man to stay on good terms with because riders of good will are welcome and he's not interested in any bounty posted on a good old boy."

She muttered, "That's what I said," with her lips against his bare chest.

Longarm said, "He's a bad man to get on bad terms with because he has so many others who want to stay on good terms with him and he only has to express annoyance with a pest to see that pest swatted. If not by the law, by another outlaw who'd as soon not have the law spoiling a good thing."

"Then this Pete Maxwell *can* be dangerous," Marmion insisted.

Longarm said, "Only when he has to be. He'd have no call to run sheep as far west as McKinely County, even if all those sheep didn't belong to the Bureau of Indian Affairs. It looks as if some troublemaker, *knowing* Don Pedro's rep, made up this rumor about him out of whole cloth. But, like I said, I'll feel better hearing as much from him, come morning. So let's see if we can get some shut-eye, doll face."

They could, and in the morning when they asked out front about breakfast they were told they were having breakfast with Don Pedro over to the big house. So that's where they headed.

The courtly Pete Maxwell was waiting for them on his front veranda, seated in a rocking chair in a white linen suit and tie that set off his slightly swarthy complexion, coal black hair and mustache, but sort of rugged, regular American features. He rose to bow and kiss Marmion's hand. (They said he'd been sent to fancy private schools.) But he never asked just what their exact relationship was. And when they went inside to find the mysterious Deluvina Maxwell presiding over a handsome breakfast table, they didn't ask about her, either.

Deluvina Maxwell was mysterious because most everyone you asked had a different tale to tell about her. She was a severely handsome woman in her early thirties who insisted upon being called La Señorita Maxwell even though she admitted to being pure Navaho. Some said she'd been left in the lurch at the Bosque Redondo agency when the Navaho were allowed to go home in '68. Some said the Maxwells had bought her off Mescalero raiders who'd kidnapped her. Nobody could explain why anybody would leave a pretty teenager with two good legs indeed behind, or how come Mescalero, who considered themselves kin to the Navaho and never fought with 'em, would have a Navaho captive to sell. Deluvina Maxwell was just there, lording it over the other Mex help, seeming to act as Don Pedro's housekeeper, play pretty, or both.

That morning she just dished out the French toast with sausage on fine china as Don Pedro heard Longarm out on the rumors concerning him and a crew of Anglo recruits.

Maxwell swore this was the first he'd heard of his mad desire for more range to the west. He said, "Makes no sense for us to expand in that direction, Longarm. I'd wind up with that big gap of cultivated bottomland along the Rio Grande between hither and yon. It would make communicating across my *partidarios* mighty complicated. For I have supervisors in high places who can't read and write. I don't recall that former Navaho range as anything worth fighting over, anyway."

Marmion arched a brow and allowed the range around her own Double W suited her just fine.

Deluvina muttered, murderously, "Hear me. My people held that land. *All* of it. Before Rope Thrower and his soldiers took it away from us."

Maxwell waved a dismissive hand to say, "I never said it wasn't *good* range, ladies. I said it was not my cup of tea. I wouldn't care to range my stock that far if nobody was disputing my right to do so and a swarm of Texas cattlemen makes for disputed range indeed!"

He speared a square of French toast with his fork as he went on, "I tried to tell that Texas Reb, John Chisum, what would happen if he tried to horn in on the Union vets who'd gotten there first. I'm still here because I stayed out of it. I mean to be here no matter how things go on the far side of the Rio Grande."

Longarm said, "I'd like to wire that cheering news to my home office, Pete. You don't have a telegraph office here at Fort Sumner, do you?"

The sheep baron who owned the place chuckled and said, "Not hardly. I can send or receive mail to Santa Fe within forty-eight hours and that's good enough for me."

Maxwell thought and decided, "Quicker if I pay a dispatch rider extra. Why don't you wire from Las Vegas on your way back to Albuquerque?"

Longarm smiled uncertainly and said, "We won't be going that far north on our way back to Albuquerque, Pete. We'll be changing stagecoaches at Santa Rosa for the run over the high country."

Maxwell asked, "How come? Do you enjoy getting spanked? That's a mighty bumpy trail from Santa Rosa west."

Longarm said, "We noticed. You know a better way?"

Maxwell said, "Sure I do. I go over to Albuquerque now and again. So I've tried her more ways than one. The mail coach up the riverside road to the rail stop at Las Vegas runs smoother at a steady average of nine miles an hour. Has you there from here in no more than twelve hours."

Longarm frowned and said, "But, Pete, that's way the hell out of our way and Lord have mercy if I don't feel dumb! You're right and how come I didn't see that?"

Maxwell said, "You're not from these parts. You know New Mexico from the map."

Marmion asked what she was missing.

Longarm said, "The stagecoach leg of his suggested return trip will involve about the same milage, along the far less bumpy cattle trail and wagon trace along the river. So we'll get in to Las Vegas a tad sooner and more comfortable than by the way we came."

She demurred, "I can see that. But isn't Las Vegas miles and miles out of our way?"

He said, "It sure is. And the train from there to Albuquerque runs forty or fifty miles an hour, to get us there in another comfortable three hours, and I could kick myself!"

Marmion laughed a skylark laugh and said, "So could I. But at least we got to meet Jim and Nancy. I wonder if they're still together."

Longarm changed the subject to save having to brag about that gunfight in the high chaparral. He asked Maxwell how long they'd have to wait for that coach to Las Vegas. When their host allowed there'd be one coming though before noon, Longarm allowed that didn't give them much more time to talk, and added he had a heap of questions about the sheep business.

Maxwell told him to finish his coffee and he'd show them around his dipping and docking operation, over beyond the peach orchard.

Marmion asked if you docked young rams the way you docked bull calves and when Maxwell allowed they surely did, she said she'd as soon wait on the veranda with Deluvina. So the two men carried on their conversation in Border Mex, which might have been rude in front of a Texas gal, along their way to nowheres much, out in the peach orchard.

Longarm asked and Maxwell assured him there was no print shop there in his private town. Longarm decided, in English, "The son of a bitch behind it all has gone from fibbing to forgery, then. Had them printed notices about you wanting help run off somewheres else by some printer. If only I can find the likely innocent printer . . ."

"What can you charge anybody with?" asked Pete Maxwell.

To which Longarm could only reply, "I was hoping nobody would ask me that. I don't suppose you'd care to press charges?"

Maxwell shrugged and asked, "Why should I? I've

never seen any of those fool HELP WANTED notices. None were ever posted over here along the Pecos and no harm's been done to me or mine."

Longarm allowed he'd seen stock castrated in his time and so he turned to go back and see if he and Marmion had time for a shower, together, before they spent another hot and dusty day on the trail.

Chapter 17

They were coated with mustard-colored dust and swearing they'd never ride another stagecoach as long as they lived when they boarded the night train at Las Vegas. The contrast betwixt the two forms of travel was one thundering wonder. As he washed up in the rolling gent's room whilst she did the same at the other end of the car, Longarm found it easier to believe those articles in the *Scientific American* predicting that someday there'd be airships carrying passengers a hundred miles an hour. He was still a young man and he remembered trains that had no running water or flush commodes.

They got into Albuquerque in the wee small hours and went upstairs to shower again for bed. When Longarm went to see how old Dodsworth was he found the room empty with the mattress rolled up.

He went back down to ask the night man why. He was told Dodsworth was in the hospital. He'd started to get better but came down with chills in place of fever. So his senior assistant, Agent Tanner, had checked him into the hospital, like it or not.

Rejoining Marmion, Longarm allowed Tanner wasn't as empty a windbag as he'd thought. Then they tore off a quickie and slept the sleep of the plumb worn-out.

Bright and early in the morning Longarm made it over to the hospital before breakfast. He found Tanner, Roberts and Hoffmann there along with the two sheepherders, MacTavish and DuVille. They were smoking in the waiting room at one end of the hall. Tanner said he'd wired Washington. He figured they'd relieve Dodsworth and appoint him in the older man's place. He didn't sound as if this worried him all that much.

Longarm told them to hold the thought and went back out in the hall to scout up the resident doc. He found the same in an office down to the far end, introduced himself, and asked how bad things were.

The resident, a shorter gent of about the same age, who seemed to be of the Hebrew persuasion, said, "Very bad. Your friend has been neglecting his own doctor's orders. It's an all-too-common mistake with malaria. Once you catch it, it never goes away. You have to take your quinine religiously as long as you live. But between bouts you feel no symptoms and may in fact feel fine. So you forget your daily dose of bitter tonic powders and when nothing happens, at first, you get cocky."

Longarm nodded and asked, "Is that how come the folk in British India develop a taste for gin and tonic water?"

The resident nodded and said, "The gin and club soda help the medicine go down. Mr. Dodsworth's been dosing himself with the newer and very bitter quinine pills. Swallow one wrong, get it stuck in your throat and you taste the gall all day."

The resident smiled wryly and added, "I think he's learned his lesson and he's been asking for you. I'll show you to him. We have him in isolation because, frankly, we don't know how malaria spreads and we'd just as soon not have any more of it in Albuquerque!"

As they went to Dodsworth's private room, Longarm asked if they had any malaria in those parts. The resident said, "Only cases from other parts who've never shaken it. They do report some new cases from farther down the Rio

Grande. It seems to rise from stagnant muddy water. But, knock on wood, the river runs muddy but fast through the upper valley."

They went in to find Dodsworth propped up in bed but looking like death warmed over. As the resident felt his brow and took his pulse the patient told Longarm, "They brought me here against my will. You have to get me out."

Before Longarm could answer, the resident said, "Mr. Dodsworth, you are not a well man. I know you feel no chills or fever *now*. You may or may not feel your irregular heartbeat. I've prescribed regular doses of tincture of foxglove along with double your usual daily dosage of quinine. We have to monitor you round the clock lest we've overdosed you."

Dodsworth complained, "Why can't you prescribe less and let me be on my way, then?"

The resident sighed and said, "Now he's a pharmacist? Listen to me, Mr. Dodsworth. You had a close call. You're not out of the woods yet. You want to let us try and put you back on your feet or would you rather walk out and drop dead somewhere else?"

Dodsworth protested, "Nonsense! I've had malaria for years!"

The resident nodded and said, "So now it's affected your heart. Knock wood, you haven't had a heart attack yet. Keep pushing your luck and . . . trust me, you will."

Longarm said, "I'd listen to him, Ed."

Dodsworth insisted, "Those Indians are waiting. They may be getting restive and preventing that was the whole point of this mission. I can't see Tanner leading a dog round a fire plug. I'm appointing you to take over in my place, Deputy Long!"

"Do it. I'll be your witness!" said the worried resident.

Longarm started to protest. But there were times to be modest and this wasn't one of them, with the know-it-all Tanner chomping at the bit down the hall. So Longarm sent for the assemblage in the waiting room and let them crowd in to listen as Dodsworth announced they were to take orders from his *segundo,* "Buck Crawford," until he was back on his feet.

Tanner was the only one who objected. He said, "If you don't think I can cut the mustard, appoint *Roberts,* here. This man is neither BIA nor an experienced sheep man!"

Dodsworth said, "Never mind who or what he is. Just do what he says until I say different."

The resident said they were exciting his patient and herded them all outside. Longarm turned to Roberts to say, "I've personal reasons not to visit the Posada Pilar near the stockyards. They don't know you there. But if you ask for Gluepants Gafferty and tell him you're a pal of old Buck Crawford, he might listen. Tell him I need experienced trail drivers with their own broncs. Tell him if he'll ride for a dollar a day through sheep shit he's to look me up at the Mountain View. Tell him if I'm not there to stick around. I got more errands to run this morning than the morning has time to spare."

They all went out front together. As Roberts headed one way and most started the other, Hoffmann asked where "Buck" was going, if not back to their hotel with them. Longarm said, "Western Union, to see if there are any answers to wires I sent out earlier. What say we all meet in the hotel taproom at noon. I'll fill you all in on anything new I know before *La Siesta* sets in. I have my own plans for *La Siesta.*"

Nobody argued. Longarm could have walked a good part of the way back along the same route. He turned off at the corner to go partly out of his way so's he could have a look at those pent-up sheep, now that he was in personal charge of the critters.

Over by the stockyards he scouted up the fodder and water foreman to order double rations for now. When the railroad man allowed it would cost them, Longarm said, "I know. Can't be helped. We may be running some fat and sweat off them woolies on the way to where we got to drive 'em. So I want them to leave here fat and sassy."

The railroad man asked when that might be.

Longarm said, "Ain't certain. But it better be soon if we don't want the U.S. Cavalry chasing more Indians this summer than planned. I'm waiting on some missing pieces I may or may not get in time to do things a tad less rough and ready."

The railroad man asked, "What if you can't?"

To which Longarm could only reply, "We'll have to try her rough and ready. A mess of itchy Indians are waiting on this stock over to Standing Rock."

They shook on that and parted friendly. Longarm ambled on to the Western Union to find, sure enough, Billy Vail had been wiring all over creation. The real Latigo Shaw had been seen the day before at the new Cheyenne Social Club, sipping suds with a cattle baron said to feel a mite pissed at homesteaders busting sod where the long horn had just replaced the roaming buffalo.

Longarm read on as he walked back to the hotel. Vail's opposite number in Santa Fe had confirmed that whilst there were more restless guns out for fun and profit in New Mexico Territory at the moment, Pete Maxwell hadn't bought any stock nor lost any stock in recent memory. Nobody in Santa Fe had actually *seen* those notorious HELP WANTED offers somebody might have printed up.

He read on, shoved the wad of telegraphs in a hip pocket and ambled on to get yoo-hooed at as he crossed the lobby, bound for the stairway to paradise, or at least another quicky before he had to meet with the boys in the taproom.

But Marmion sat fully dressed in that same corner with old Banker Forbes and a smaller somewhat younger gal with light brown hair almost matching her whipcord riding habit.

As Longarm joined them, Marmion introduced the younger gal as a Clora Taylor of the T Bar Zero, a couple of spreads along the Rio Puerco from her own Rocking M. Marmion said, "It's getting way out of hand. Tell him, Clora."

The brown-haired gal said, "Angus Glourie has formed a vigilance committee of like-minded riders, sworn to make a stand against all comers, including the Territorial Guard or damnyankee colored Cavalry down to Fort Stanton before they let one head of mutton show its bleating face out our way!"

Longarm said, "Last I heard, most of the Ninth Cavalry out of Stanton were riding with the Tenth, chasing Mescalero."

Clora nodded and said, "My dad says Angus is counting on that, for all his brave talk."

Marmion explained, "Clora came home from college to run things when her mother died and her father had a stroke."

Clora said, "I guess my dad still knows a thing or two. He says if he could get his right leg and gun hand to work like it used to he'd show Angus up as the four flusher he was born. Dad says he knows Angus and that sass he rides for, Judith Morrison, are just like that loud-mouthed John Chisum who encouraged green furriners to fight the county machine and was nowhere to be seen when the bullets commenced to fly!"

Banker Forbes said, "That could be their game. I understand from my friendly rivals in the mortage and loan line that after the dust settled Big John's Jingle Bob herd included the stock of lesser ranchers ruined on both sides."

Longarm said, "This may be none of my beeswax, but might your bank hold paper on Miss Judith Morrison and her hotheaded neighbors?"

Forbes said, "Of course. Most all the stockmen over that way have taken out improvement loads against beef futures. How much beef do you expect them to sell in the middle of a range war?"

Longarm grimaced and said, "Not much. Had Tunstall and McSween *lived* they'd have wound up outlawed. Uncle John Chisum might have gone down the rapids with 'em had not he noticed in time that his pipe dreams of wresting army beef contracts from a retired field grade officer who still drank with the boys out to Fort Stanton needed study."

He shrugged and added, "On the other hand, other Texas stockmen might have studied some afore they rode off to a cause that was lost from the first shot fired at Fort Sumner. There's a certain breed of swaggering know-it-all who seems ever willing to fire that first shot."

Banker Forbes suggested getting in touch with Governor Wallace, up in Santa Fe.

Longarm grimaced and replied, "Ain't got the time old Lew's likely to use on proclamations and negotiations. When they sent him out here as the Lincoln County War was winding down for lack of leadership or funding, the new governor spent as long talking about what had happened as it had taken to happen. He did a good job. His general amnesty has kept the peace betwixt responsible adults. But them Navaho over to Standing Rock ain't likely to give us more than a few more days and it would take Lew Wallace more like a month to decide on the wording of his riot act. He's a caution for writing, you know. Took him two volumes to tell the tale of Ben Hur, which I could sum up in less'n ten pages."

He glanced over at the Regulator brand clock above the hotel desk to decide, "I've called another meeting in the taproom. Are you . . . still staying here at the Mountain View, Miss Marmion?"

She smiled up innocently to reply, "Of course. They have my room number at the desk if you need me later. Clora, here, will be staying at the home of Mr. Forbes for now."

Clora Taylor said, "Not longer than overnight. I have to get back out to our home spread. My dear old dad may need me."

"Don't you have any hired help?" Longarm asked.

She said, "Of course. But they're young and . . . from Texas. I have to make sure they stay on the straight and narrow with Angus Glourie out to stir things up."

Seeing they had that much time to work with, Longarm allowed he'd get in touch with her through Marmion if he had anything new for her to take home with her. Then he ambled into the nearby taproom to find most of the others already there lined up along the bar.

The red-bearded Hamish MacTavish had changed into an even wilder outfit. Chaps might make sense riding through chaparral, but goat skin chaps with the hair still on?

The bowlegged Scot had scouted up a brace of six guns to wear with his big, white, ten-gallon hat. He indicated Agent Roberts with a thumb and said, "We're about to be joined by cowboys and I'll noo hae any mon laughing at me. Sae I'd dressed for the occasion, ye ken."

Roberts said, "Your friend, Gluepants, thinks he might be able to get us a score of experienced drovers willing to hold their noses for a dollar a day this far from the fall roundup of serious stock. I told him to report to you, here, either way."

MacTavish opined, "Och, I doubt a mere score of cattle drovers will be able to hold six thousand sheep together. But I'm willing to gie it a try, ye ken."

Longarm took a deep breath, let half of it out so his voice wouldn't crack and soberly said, "You won't be riding with us, whoever you may be."

He'd expected the imposter to insist he was Hamish MacTavish of the Mull of Kintyre, but the red-bearded Scot moved fast as thought, without expression, and had both six-guns clear of their holsters before Longarm's first round doubled him over to catch the second round through the crown of his new hat.

Neither the hat nor the man who'd said he was Hamish MacTavish looked all that pristine as they lay at Longarm's feet on the sawdust covered floor.

They spread sawdust on the floors of taprooms to soak up spilled drinks. But the sawdust they'd spread that morning was filling in for the sawdust on the floor of your average butcher shop.

Chapter 18

The loud-mouthed Tanner was the first to come unstuck. He gasped, "Why did you just shoot MacTavish down like a dog, goddamn it?"

Agent Rogers snorted, "Where were you, just now? Didn't you see the loser slap leather first?"

Longarm said, "He wasn't Hamish MacTavish. I was hoping to take him alive and ask him who the hell he was. What the law on both sides of the Atlantic knows for certain is still circumstantial."

Reporter Phalen of the *Santa Fe Weekly Democrat* had followed his nose for news in the direction of nearby gunplay. So he came in just as Longarm was explaining, "The real Hamish MacTavish boarded the steam ship *Thistlegorm* to sail down the Clyde with his sheepdogs in a second-class but private cabin.

"They got off with this mysterious cuss at Alexandria, with the passport of Hamish MacTavish, to show up for the job MacTavish had applied for with the U.S. Department of Agriculture."

Hoffmann said, "We've extended such invitations to foreign experts. Next to Basques, Scots are supposed to know more about sheep and sheepdogs than most."

Longarm reloaded as he said, "Whatever. The passengers were long gone and the ship's crew was cleaning up when they found this dead body down in the bilge. They figured it was a stowaway. There were no visible marks, so they figured he'd taken a bad fall, dodging the deck watch in rough seas. When they cabled the news home it turned out the Glasgow Police had traced a desperate, quick-thinking killer to the dock area and lost him. So up until Marshal Billy Vail of the Denver District Court inspired some second thoughts, they figured one Red Sweeny Skane had dyed his hair black, stowed away on an outward-bound steamer and come to a bad end in heavy weather."

A pair of uniformed local roundsmen came in, guns drawn, as Longarm calmly declared, "Once cables commenced to compare notes with an ocean between, it didn't take long to determine that the real Hamish MacTavish was six feet tall with dark hair, the same as the body they had on its way home on ice. Red Sweeny Skane, as anyone here can see, was a short, bowlegged cuss with red hair and a beard to match."

He nodded at the local lawman and said, "What I have to say next is better said in private. You'd better come along with us, Reporter Phalen. Things have started to get delicate around here."

Leaving everyone else to marvel at the remains on the floor, Longarm led the copper badges and local reporter into the alley and over to that secluded corner under the paper palm tree before he produced his true colors in the form of his badge, his federal deputy's warrant and that letter of authorization from their local judge.

As the three of them were still wising up, he told Reporter Phalen, "The U.S. Bill of Rights forbids my shoving a gag in your press, pard. But how do you feel about a scoop that will make this apprehension of a single killer on the dodge look less important by far?"

As he'd hoped, Reporter Phalen said he'd sell most anything but his immortal soul for a real scoop. So Longarm told him to hold the thought as he tidied things up with the copper badges. They allowed it was no skin off their noses if Longarm wanted to give the credit to some bounty hunter called Buck Crawford, as long as he had carte blanche from their own superiors to conduct his investigation as he saw fit.

As they secured the death scene for the coroner's crew, Longarm told Reporter Phalen how he wanted the story "slanted" in the extra his paper would be putting out ahead of time. He didn't need to explain to a professional newspaper man how you could make things read a mite awry without printing any downright lies.

Phalen gravely suggested he had every right to *presume* details Buck Crawford hadn't said right out. Once he'd caught on to Longarm's drift he said, "Leave it to me. What else would Buck Crawford be but a bounty hunter with a private license? He's not riding for any federal court as a regular lawman, is he?"

They shook on it and the reporter lit out to file his scoop without waiting for the meat wagon to arrive.

Longarm went up to his room to touch bases with Marmion. She wasn't there. She'd left a note on the dresser, saying she and Clora Taylor would both be spending the night at the Forbes house in town and asking him to understand, darling.

He was glad she felt that way. He figured to be busy as a one-armed paper hanger in a wind storm for the next few hours, siesta time or not.

He went back down to find the mess cleaned up but the taproom still abuzz. He retired to the dining room and ordered a light snack of steak smothered in chili to settle his flutters and give himself something to do besides smoke.

As he'd hoped, Gluepants Gafferty paid no mind to *La Siesta* and he came in just after noon with Agent Roberts. Longarm made a mental note that Roberts neither argued nor shilly-shallied. He ordered coffee for the both of them and told Gluepants, "Our offer for drovers still stands at a dollar a day and found. *You'll* get twice that for riding herd

157

on them. We figure less than a week on the trail to Standing Rock. Think you could stand the smell that long for that much?"

Gluepants said, "Cutting off strays and holding a herd of *geese* in a bunch for that long ain't a big deal. Asking men to get shot at for a dollar a day is a big deal, Buck."

Longarm said, "I know. Ain't planning on shooting our way through them eighty miles or so of disputed range. Planning on getting those hotheads to see the light, or if they won't see the light, blindfold 'em some. If you're in, we'd best put our heads together with our two sheep experts, Hoffmann and DuVille. I want them reading over my shoulder as I lay out the drive I'm fixing to plan."

Roberts asked, "What about Tanner?"

Longarm started to say something cutting, decided he wasn't the one to fire Indian agents who didn't work for him and said, "All right, him too. Those other sheepherders Dodsworth sent for have had time enough to get here and we won't be *walking* them sheep like poodle dogs. I just now ordered extra fodder and water for the herd. Aim to head 'em out rested up and soggy enough to cover some ground without stopping more than once an hour for no more than a nibble if they can find it. By the time they're turned over to the Indians at Standing Rock, they'll be desperately hating our guts. Some might not make it. Most of them ought to."

Gluepants said, "Fuck the sheep. How can I assure my pals you ain't out to get them all shot? The most dangerous job I've ever had was aboard some mean mustangs. I ain't no gun waddie. The boys I might be able to recruit ain't, neither."

Longarm nodded and said, "Gun-toting stock thieves run off a dozen head at a time. They ain't the sort of riders we need for a serious drive. I'll handle any shooting as needs to take place."

Gluepants started to snort in derision. Then he decided, "Well, I was there when you sent them *Rurales* into early retirement and Roberts, here, told me about more recent events in the taproom across the lobby. But we've been told this hardcase Angus Glourie has gathered a force of fifty or more!"

Longarm said, "Fifty or more *cowhands,* if that many. Those Texans never took that Indian land from the Indians, personal. They filed for land and water rights with the Interior Department, civilized as anybody."

Gluepants said, "We heard-tell they've sent out away for hired guns."

Longarm said, "I know. I'm one of them. I've been playing a two-faced part with that bunch. I'll be heading over yonder to see if I can get us out of needless gunplay before any of you shove one sheep across the Rio Grande. The bottomlands far as, say, the crossroads cluster called Last Chance, hard two hours to the north west of here, ain't disputed by anybody."

Gluepants said, "I've been over yonder. To a barn dance. There's this general store cum post office and that big barn they use for hoedowns and as a grange hall. Right?"

Longarm said, "So the map says. Last Chance is near the Rio Puerco where it runs north to south. The bigger claims tend to lie along the Puerco and Arroyo Chico. Both upstream from Last Chance. Anyone can see, and they have, how easy it would be for us to run them sheep along the left bank of the Arroyo Chico around that big old mesa, moving slow but smoothly into the high country closer to the divide. Bust loose from that long drink of water where it's running north instead of east and you can beeline over the rolling, well-watered grasslands beyond to where the waters run the other way and it ain't that far from Standing Rock."

Gluepants nodded and asked, "In sum, the sort of prime grazing cattlemen and sheep men kill each other over!"

Longarm polished off the last of his steak, leaving some of the chili for the flies out back, and said, "Let's go up and gather the others as I lay out my next moves in more detail. It's a pain in the ass to say the same things over and over."

So they did, gathered in Longarm's room, and if anybody wondered why there was a hint of raspberry scent in the air, they never said so.

By the time their meeting broke up, it was too hot to go outside without a damned good reason. Gluepants did, having a reason. The rest of them repaired to their own hotel rooms to strip and flop a spell. Longarm lay wistful atop the covers, with his old organ grinder rising reproachfully as he indulged in scandalous daydreams involving Judy, Pilar, Marmion and, as long as she was in town, that brown-haired Clora Taylor. What a gal didn't know you were thinking about her could hardly be held against you.

Later that afternoon Longarm went back to the hospital alone to fill old Dodsworth in on how things were going. Dodsworth insisted it was too soon to move 'em out. He demanded, "What if you wind up with sheep scattered from hell to breakfast in those hills?"

Longarm said, "You'll get to blame me. If we get 'em all safe and sound to Standing Rock, you can take the credit. I don't want to go down in history as a famous sheepherder."

Dodsworth laughed weakly and allowed those dawdling replacements were hardly inspirational. Then he asked Longarm if he'd ask the nurse for an extra blanket.

Longarm did and went on his way, wishing there was two or more of him as the shadows lengthened and the streets started coming back to life.

He ambled over to Banker Forbes's new house, which sported a mansard roof of copper above adobe walls. The banker's surprisingly comely Mex wife and little brown-haired Clora were out back, snapping peas like old pals. Clora said Marmion and the banker had gone to see some judge Forbes knew to file a deposition with him. She said he'd asked her to make up a list of the hotheads backing Judith Morrison and her pet shootist, Angus Glourie. Banker Forbes had said that once blood was spilled it would be important to have it on record who'd been for and who'd been against the war. She said most of her neighbors out to the northwest were for peace or no more than sullen silence and voting Democrat, come fall. Forbes had told them how folk who'd tried to stay neutral had been ruined in other range wars.

Longarm said, "That's about the size of it. I'm hoping to stave off any serious gunplay by getting out yonder well in advance of any sheep. By now you know as well as Marmion and Banker Forbes that there ain't no big sheep outfit trying to move in on your cattle country. All I have to do is convince the foolish or those just spoiing for adventure that it ain't nice to peg shots at your Uncle Sam if you aim to graze any sort of stock on public land."

He glanced out at the low sun to the west and added, "Reckon I'd best go saddle up. Marmion tells me most of the speeches have been made in and around that Last Chance stop just this side of your new holdings along the Rio Puerco."

She nodded and said, "That's about the hub of the trouble. Lots of cattle folk farther out have barely paid any mind to Angus and his gun waddies strutting and wardancing around the grange hall. Do you want me to ride along and introduce you to the folk out yonder? Might save some tense discussion if they knew right off you knew me and Marmion."

Longarm started to say what came natural to a man riding off into a great unknown with twilight coming on. But he sensed the little brown-haired gal had common sense to go with her belongings out yonder in the first place. So he said he'd go saddle up and meet her there before sundown. She said she'd go back to the hotel with him, because that was where she'd left her own mount.

When they got there her pony turned out to be a Spanish barb with a coat that harmonized with her whipcord riding habit. Being a gal who ran a cattle spread for her dad, she naturally rode astride in her split skirts. He noticed the braided leather throw-rope and Winchester saddle gun that went with her center-fire dally roping saddle, as well.

They forded the Rio Grande where the stage route to Gallup advised them to and swung up Coon Road as the sun was setting. They caught the post road to Last Chance to ride along in the gloaming.

Clora took the lead and set a mile-eating pace at a trot. Longarm admired riders who could stand in the stirrups and take the punishment that was easier on one's mount. It bespoke some time in the saddle on her way to womanhood.

They walked 'em some and trotted 'em some and a couple of hours on Clora waved her riding quirt at dots of light ahead to declare that was Last Chance.

He was glad he'd let her tag along as they rode into the crossroads. A whole lot of ponies were tethered all around and the mostly male crowd around the open entrance to the barnlike grange hall seemed loaded for bear and on the prod. But they eased up some as Clora introduced Longarm as a pal while he tethered their own mounts out front.

Once he had, they went on in, where some gals were mixed in and a long trestle table under hanging lanterns had been spread with jugs and snacks from the general store across the way.

Clora allowed she'd have a pull at one of the jugs but then, as they'd planned along the way out, she allowed she had to get on up the river and see to her dear old dad.

As she lit out, the raven-haired Judith Morrison came through the crowd with the black-clad Angus Glourie looming behind her. She smiled up at Longarm uncertainly to say, "We've been wondering about you, ah, Buck. You seem to have gotten in awfully tight with those sheepherding rascals in town."

As Longarm intended, ears all around perked up as he replied in a not-too-friendly tone, "You told me to get in tight with them. That was our deal. As you'll see in the papers, if you ain't already heard, I just flimflammed a good excuse to shoot another blamed sheepherder. So with them

162

three I shot earlier, you owe me four hundred dollars. That's how come I rode out here. Talk is cheap. But I want my money. How come I had to ride all the way out here to ask for my money? What are you all trying to pull on me, Miss Judy?"

Chapter 19

The beautiful but imperious brunette blinked, "Pull on you? I don't understand, ah, Buck."

He said, "You can cut the Buck stuff, now. Them BIA agents know who I am. I had to show my range detective's hunting license after I shot that last sheepherder and a reporter for the *Santa Fe Weekly Democrat* was there. He'd heard of me and knew my rep. So there went my job as a sheepherder. But I've shot four of 'em and their leader's all stove up in the hospital. I ain't charging you for him, since you said it would be five hundred if I finished him off. But I've done all I can and it's time to ride on. So pay me my four hundred and we'll say no more about it."

Angus Glourie said, "Hold on. There was nothing in the papers about those Mexicans you shot it out with being sheepherders. Way *we* heard was that you got into a personal grudge fight with 'em."

Longarm sneered, "As Buck Crawford, working for the very sheep outfit Miss Judy, here, asked me to head off. What was I supposed to tell the infernal law, that I was a rider for the cattleman's protective association called Latigo Shaw who shot Mex sheepherders whenever I could manage? What are you all trying to pull? Two Ton Tobin told me you were respectable stock growers, not carnival

165

grifters. Miss Judy, here, made me what she said was your standing offer and I shot your blamed sheepherders. So where's my damn money? Sorry, ladies."

He had some mutters going in the crowd by now. Somebody, bless him, told a pal, "Heard-tell of Latigo Shaw coming down from Wyoming to dance the hoolihan. From what I've heard about him, I'd *pay* him."

Judith Morrison smiled murderously up at the gun she'd bragged on hiring to more than one pal present and said, "Nobody is out to welsh on our deal, Latigo. Your barging in on me with that surly attitude just took me aback. You'll get your money, for heaven's sake."

"When?" asked Longarm, in the same attitude, adding, "Two Ton Tobin told me most of you all were Scotch. He didn't tell me you were *Lowland* Scots."

As he'd hoped, that hit a nerve in more than one gathered round. Two Ton Tobin hadn't told him shit, but Longarm knew there was a bone of contention betwixt Lowland and Highland Scots, with each accusing the other of being the tight Scotsman of music hall jokes. The Highlanders, which included most sheep-hating Texican Scots, bragged on being free spenders and generous to a fault.

Judith knew what some might be thinking. She smiled sweet as honey laced with blue vitriol and said, "For heaven's sake, did you think I carry that kind of money *on* me, Latigo? I was speaking in the name of our central committee when I made you our standing offer. I have to get the money from *them*, see?"

Longarm looked around the crowded barn to reply, "Not hardly. Where are they if they got my money? I got to *ride*, girl. Lord only knows how long the story I told about that last sheepherder might hold up."

A lanky Texan wearing his holsters tied down asked what "Latigo" had told them in town about that sheepherder he'd shot.

Longarm samiled thinly and replied, "I said he was *wanted*, of course. My private license ain't good for plain old sheepherders, more's the pity. I said I had it on good authority he was wanted over in his old country for a killing and that's why I had to kill him."

Then he said, "No offense, but I never rode out here to explain my own ways and means. I've done more than I ever agreed to about them sheep. I doubt you all will ever see any blamed sheep out this way. I'm still waiting to see the money I have coming for services damn well rendered. Sorry, ladies."

He waited for an answer as Judith and Angus went on whispering. Then he asked, "How come this secret committee don't attend its own meetings if it aims to have a war with the government?"

Judith Morrison said, "Because it's a *secret* committee, of course. I'm sending my segundo, here, to fetch your money, Latigo. Simmer down and don't be such a grouch. Have something to eat and drink. Calm down and take it easy 'til he gets back."

"Where's he going?" asked "Latigo," suspiciously.

She laughed and said, "That's for us to know and nobody else to find out. Our leaders have warned us there could be trouble with the land office if that big sheep outfit is really tied in with the BIA."

She nudged Angus and told him he'd best get cracking. So Angus left, in a snit of his own.

Knowing how many others were listening, Longarm warily asked Judith, "What big outfit might we be talking about, Miss Judy? I told you early on, in town, that herd of sheep had been assembled by the BIA to grade up the Navaho flocks."

The tied-down holsters said, "Come on, Latigo, everybody knows Pete Maxwell, that half-breed sheep baron along the Pecos, has been hiring on extra help for a bodacious sheep drive west."

Longarm shook his head and said, "That's what I heard, too. So I spent more uncomfortable time than I had to spare, riding over to Fort Sumner and back. Nobody there had seen any of them wonderous HELP WANTED posters Maxwell is supposed to have printed up. There ain't no printing shop over to Fort Sumner, by the way."

A short stubby member of the crowd asked, "Then how do you explain *this*?" as he produced what looked something like a reward poster with the HELP WANTED set in fancy letters, like you saw on patent medicine.

Longarm took the poster, noting it was printed on bond paper as he held it up to the light. He said, "This sure looks real. But some troublemaker's gone to a whole lot of trouble or everybody I talked to over to Fort Sumner ought to go on the wicked stage. Can I hold on to this? I know this newspaper man who might be able to tell me where I'd go to have something like this printed."

The stubby cuss, who was naturally curious, said, "Sure. I got more at home. But why would anybody advertise for extra help if nobody was out to hire extra help?"

Longarm shrugged and said, "Whoever done it must have had some reason."

Then he turned away and ambled over to the buffet table. Judith tagged along after him as the crowd got to buzzing some. He'd been hoping it might. It beat all how stubborn minds you coudn't budge with the simple truth could think for themselves if you set them to thinking.

Staring down at the cold cuts, pickles and pastries laid out under the flickering coal oil lanterns, Longarm marveled, "Will you look at all them whores' ovaries! Guess that committee was planning on riders coming in from far and wide."

Judith said, "I think *hors d'oeuvres* was the term you had in mind and Latigo, we have to talk."

Longarm said, "I'm listening," as he commenced to build himself a salami sandwich with the sliced cheese instead of bread on the outside.

She said, "I mean alone. Why don't we . . . take a little stroll along the river in the moonlight?"

Longarm said, "I like it in here where I can see who's sneaking up on me. No offense. Some old boys cotton more than me to willful gals who blow hot and cold, Miss Judy. I rode out here for my money, not no moonlight nor moonshine."

Knowing others were listening, he threw in, "How come your *segundo* has to ride so far to meet with your committee? What are all these others doing here if your leadership is somewheres else?"

A bitchy she-male voice in the crowd—there was always a gal like that in any crowd—asked her own escort, "What about that, Hiram? You said Angus Glourie had called a big meeting here and all of a sudden it seems he's just an errand boy! Who's running this show if it's not your peerless leader, Angus?"

And so it went, with time flying when you were having fun. Longarm had noticed, standing the death watch with old boys fixing to hang in the morning, how the sands of time seemed to run so much faster when you were in no hurry for things to happen. Longarm had set out to stall for as much time as he could manage, out this way. Knowing he was surrounded by suspicious minds and restless guns made every minute he could stall seem precious, and hence hard to hang on to.

Judith tried in vain to get him away from the others as more and more of the others wondered aloud about things they hadn't thought about before.

Longarm played them like skittish trout on a cobweb line, offering no obvious contradictions to the tales they'd been told as he let men with contrary notions but common sense ask one another the questions they might have asked in the first damned place.

Judith wasn't the only gal there who flirted with him some and others said they wanted to go home as the night wore on and nothing happened.

A few went along with that notion. Most stayed put, long past the bedtimes of country folk, sensing something might be up, if they only stayed up a spell. For this meeting, up to now, hadn't gone the way any of them had expected.

Then, as Judith had predicted, her *segundo* came in, looking as if he'd been riding hard, to hand her, not Longarm, a fat paper envelope.

Judith asked if Longarm wanted to count it. He allowed he surely did. As others crowded round the sight of ten dollar silver certificates being tallied by lantern light, Glourie blurted, "What happened to all them sheep? When I rode past the stockyards all them pens were empty in the moonlight. How come?"

Longarm put the envelope away as he mildy replied, "This secret bunch you're only fronting for meets in town, pard? I had the impression they were cattlemen, too."

Judith looked as if she wanted to rip Glourie's tongue out by the roots. The *segundo* snapped, "Never mind who's fronting for whomsoever. Asked you about all them sheep, not where I've just been."

Longarm smiled and replied, "Did you see any sheep in this child's company when he rode in with Miss Clora Taylor? Did you overtake any sheep as you were riding back from town just now? Are you sure there was ever any sheep you really had to worry about? What sort of games have you and somebody with access to a print shop in town been playing on everybody out this way, Glourie?"

The black-clad *segundo* gasped, "Just what might you be accusing me of, you accusing cuss?"

Longarm said, "Since you ask. Somebody's been lying to these folk, and it hasn't been me."

There came a collective gasp. The Rocking M rider called Slats said, "Sounds to me as if he just called you a liar, Angus."

Glourie hissed, "I got ears, goddamn it. You want to take that back or fill your fist, Latigo Shaw?"

Longarm stepped clear of the trestle table, smiling, to calmly reply, "Ain't taking nothing back. Doubt I'll be called upon to fill my fist. I don't think you have the sand, sonny."

That bitchy gal in the crowd jeered, "I don't, neither. Go for your gun and show us what you're made of, Angus!"

Judy Morrison told her to shut up. But the damage was done. Another voice called out, "I'm offering two to one he crawfishes!"

There were no takers. Glourie stammered, "Hold on, he's packing a license to shoot folk. I'm just a ranch foreman. I ain't allowed to shoot folk!"

Yet another man there jeered, "That ain't what you've been saying up to now, Angus Glourie! Up to now you've been saying you're the bees' knees with a gun and no man to cross. So what are you fixing to do about this one man alone calling you a liar to your face?"

Angus Glourie sobbed, "I sure ain't fixing to stick around where I don't seem to have a friend in the bunch!"

And then he was gone, chased out the door by taunts and laughter. The tied-down holsters told Longarm, "Always thought he talked too much for a man who'd seen the elephant. I rode under General Hood in the war and I've never been one to say I could lick any man in the house."

Longarm said, "Nobody who's seen the elephant ever does. I've no intent to start up with any man who doesn't start up with me. Have you tried them pickled pigs' feet with that fancy French mustard? It'll cut any phlegm in your throat better than cough medicine."

But the crowd was already breaking up, with more than one wife asking her man what in tarnation that had all been about. Longarm wanted to hold everyone there a spell. So naturally he found himself nigh alone with Judith Morrison as the lanterns commenced to sputter.

He smiled down at her to say, "Well, I thank you for the bounty money and I reckon I'll be headed back to town, seeing it's over, Miss Judy."

She pleaded, "Ride out to my Rocking M with me. We have so much to talk about, Latigo."

He shook his head and insisted, "I said it's over. I know you and a lot of the other hotheads were just being used. I told you early on you had no just cause for a head-on collision with the BIA and your good old Uncle Sam. You wouldn't listen because you were too stirred up to listen. But in times to come you'll thank me for what I done."

"What have you done for us?" she asked, adding, "I really want to know. I'm trying to understand, darling!"

He said, "It's too early to say and I ain't your darling. I ain't even the man you mistook me for but all's well as ends well and this ain't your money I'm keeping for my time and trouble."

He laughed, kissed her in a brotherly way, and added, "Not that it wasn't a lot of fun."

Then he was outside, mounting up, as Judith stood flusterpated in the doorway, calling, "Come back here, damn you! I'm not the sort of woman a man can just have his way with and ride off like an infernal tomcat!"

She was wrong, of course. He found it easy as hell to ride off without even thinking of looking back. The night was clear and Dancer pranced him back to town in less than two hours. So it was still dark when he reined into the alley behind his hotel and dismounted to lead her on to the stable.

Then Clora Taylor was yelling, "Custis! Behind you!" and he let go the reins to sidestep as he turned and drew. Angus Glourie got off the shot he'd been aiming to put in Longarm's back, and then Longarm's hot lead froze his guts as it staggered him back to bounce off an adobe wall and land face down in the alley grit.

Kicking the fallen man's gun clear, Longarm rolled him on his back to say, "You didn't have to do that, you fool. I didn't have any charges against you that would have stuck. You never hurt nobody with all your vainglorious threats. You were being used as a tool all the time."

"What . . . happened?" Glourie croaked, staring up.

Longarm answered, not unkinly. "Weren't you there? I had Miss Clora following you around this evening. Told her to wait for me, here at the hotel."

He called out, "Where are you at, Miss Clora?"

The little brown-haired gal came down the alley, saying, "Waiting for to see what he'd try next, Deputy Long. That last move was the only one that surprised me."

Chapter 20

It seemed doubtful Angus Glourie heard the last of their exchange. By the time the colored night manager of the stable came out with a lantern, Glourie lay dead as a turd in a milk bucket. When Longarm asked polite the stable man ager set the lantern down by the cadaver and went after Dancer, who was spooked and quivering at the far end of the fortunately blind alley. He led her inside just before a two-man night patrol came in from the other end, attracted by the gunplay at that hour.

Figuring they might, Longarm had holstered his re-loaded six-gun and pinned his badge on. As the local lawmen joined him and the brown-haired gal Longarm said, "There are times to act cute and there are times honesty works better. I'd be Deputy U.S. Marshal Custis Long, whatever else you may have heard. I've leveled with this young lady, Miss Clora Taylor of the T Bar Zero, for the same reason. Nobody can be everywhere at once. The poor unfortunate on the ground would be Angus Glourie of the Rocking M. He wanted to be known as a bad man. He was being used as a tool by a badder man and mastermind. His more criminal confederates are still at large. I ain't ready to move in on 'em yet. So how discreet can we be about this, seeing it's your call as the local jurisdiction?"

The flattered copper badges told him to just leave the matter in their discreet hands and said old Angus would still be in their morgue whenever Longarm might need him. So Longarm took Clora by one elbow and got her out of there before it could get more crowded.

As they ducked through a side entrance to the hotel, Clora asked how come they couldn't wake the real villains up and arrest them. She reminded him he'd told her she could be at the kill if things worked out the way he expected. She said, "I almost fell off my bronc when you told me on the way to Last Chance who you really were and what you suspected. But when I shadowed Angus like you asked me it all turned out just the way you said it might and when are we fixing to move in on the sneaks?"

Longarm said, "Not for some time. Have you ever baked one of them egg soufflés, Miss Flora?"

She sniffed, "Of course I have. I guess I know my way around a kitchen."

He said, "Then you know how the soufflé you spent so much time on can bust like a bubble and sink to mush if you take it out of the oven ahead of time. I got some last loose ends to tie up and I don't want to let the mastermind know what I've been up to until it's too late for him to counter a few simple moves I've made."

He thought and said, "I reckon it'll be safe to play the endgame no more than forty-eight hours down the line."

Clora almost wailed, "Forty-eight hours! I'm fixing to drop in my tracks if I don't get some sleep tonight! Where are we going to hole up together for forty-eight hours, Deputy Long?"

He started to say something dumb. Then he said, "My friends call me Custis, Miss Clora. I got a room upstairs. I mean to stay off the streets as much as possible. If you don't want to ride on home for a spell I can see about getting you another room here at the Mountain View."

She coyly suggested it ran contrary to her Scotch

thrift to hire two room when they might really get by with one.

He asked her if she was sure, pointing out he'd be headed back to Denver by the end of the week. She took his arm and grinned up at him like a mean little kid to remark, "In that case, time's a wasting, Custis."

So they just went up the back stairs without bothering the night clerk and she was peeling off her riding habit by the time he'd shut and barred the door.

She asked him not to strike a light as she beat him into bed. So he didn't. But as they got right down to country matters Longarm wondered why. For the little brown-haired gal was built like one of those Greek statues, albeit sort of pint-sized. She was a tad taller but way softer than Pilar had been. Picturing Clora sandwiched betwixt the taller Judy or Marmion inspired feelings she sensed as he eased it in all the way.

She moaned, "Me, too. I only expected this to feel *wonderful*."

So, seeing she could take it to the roots, despite her smaller frame, a grand time was had by all as they got to know one another better.

In point of fact Longarm had gotten to know Clora Taylor well indeed, even with time out for sleeping, eating and some errands he had to run during *La Siesta* the next day when not too many folk would be watching.

Then, at long last Longram got the one telegram he'd been waiting for and went back to the hotel to tell Clora, "We won. Get dressed and you can watch as I spring my egg soufflé on your false-hearted friends."

Sitting up naked in bed, an inspiring sight by broad daylight, even when you'd explored all she had to offer, more than once, Clora sighed and asked, "Does that mean . . . this is over, too, Custis?"

He didn't answer.

She softly said, "I wasn't expecting it to feel this way.

I've never planned on settling down as a stockman's woman on a dusty spread. I came home from college long enough to see to my poor sick dad. But not to stay forever and when . . . it's over, I mean to go back to the bright lights and carefree ways of San Francisco."

He said, "You told me as much, our first night together, kitten."

She said, "I'm sorry. I'm trying to be a big brave girl. Could you do me, one more time, before I get dressed?"

He started to argue. But seeing she'd saved his life and helped him crack the case, it seemed only right to dog style her 'til she begged for mercy.

After that they both got dressed to head over to Banker Forbes' house and, seeing Longarm had banked on it being the Sabbath, they found the banker seated out back on the patio, digesting his supper, along with his Mex wife and, of course, Marmion MacEwen.

Marmion looked up to gasp, "Clora! Buck! Where have you two been all this time?"

Longarm said, "Shacked up. Had to give six-thousand head of sheep time to get to Standing Rock. By now they're well on their way."

His announcement even startled Clora. She said, "You never told me anything about those sheep, Custis. Angus Glourie said they were all gone the last time he looked!"

Longarm told her, "Two can keep a secret if one of them is dead, honey lamb. As I was riding out to buy some time at Last Chance the pals I was really in with were herding them down the river to cross way south of here. Their boss, Ed Dodsworth, was against it the first time I suggested it. Said it would be out of the way. He was right. It was out of the way. Only nobody disputed their passage as they just drove 'em due west. By now they're too far west for any sore losers to head 'em off, even if they felt dumb enough for a fight with the Indian police on reservation land."

Longarm smiled wolfishly down at the banker as he

added, "So it's over. The trouble you were out to stir up never happened and you are in a whole lot of trouble."

Forbes tried, "What are you talking about? What trouble?"

Marmion asked in an imploring tone, "What are you accusing him of, darling? What's this about you and Clora, here?"

Longarm said, "You couldn't trick her and her hands into joining that stand against the U.S. government and when I noticed she had good sense I had her watching the transfer of funds as she backed my suspicions."

Marmion's tone dropped ten degrees as she asked, "Is that what you call fucking little tramps, whoever you may be?"

Longarm said, "The two of you have known all along who I was and what was really going on. You were out to establish good character with me for the land management office. Somebody who could still do business with the land office had to be out yonder as your hotheaded neighbors got rounded up or driven out of the territory."

Banker Forbes said, "Tommy rot! Why would we want people owing money to us evicted from their claims?"

Longarm said, "Thanks for establishing Miss Marmion, here, as your partner. You meant to forclose on their land and water rights when they couldn't keep up their payments, of course. Over the years they've paid all the interest and a heap of the capital. So you . . ."

"So you don't know shit about homestead claims!" the banker cut in, adding, "Should the land office foreclose on rights claimed under the Homestead Act of 1863 the property and all improvements revert to the federal government, not a mortgage holder, you sap!"

Longarm nodded and said, "That's how come no bank will issue a mortgage on an unproven homestead claim. For the first five years everything you just said holds true. But them Texas folk moved into that Indian land more than five years ago. They'd proven their claims and held free title to their land and water rights before you loaned them a dime. Like I said, you've gotten a lot of your money back, but being a greedy hog, you wanted everything. So when some hotheads got exited about rumors you and Miss Marmion, here, saw the chance to consolidate a mess of modest holdings into a cattle barony to rival Uncle John Chisum's. Using much the same methods. You figured to whip up another disasterous range war and pick up the pieces, cheap."

He fished out a folded HELP WANTED poster and went on, "A newspaper pal of mine had no trouble tracing this to a print shop using that fancy type. When I pointed out they'd done nothing wrong by running some up for you they agreed to testify against you before the banking commission."

The banker looked as if he was fixing to throw up. Longarm explained for the ladies present, "The murdersome plot to get a heap of folk shot, jailed or running was foiled before anyone on either side was hurt as a direct result. Nobody I shot but Hamish Glourie was taking orders from anyone here and Angus managed to get shot on his own. Nobody told him to backshoot me. I was supposed to tell the powers that be how these swell kids made every effort to prevent bloodshed."

He reached for a smoke as he continued, "Malicious mischief, however spiteful, calls for a slap on the wrist in criminal court and I got better places to be. So I've dropped a line to the banking commission in Santa Fe and they shall see what they shall see as they examine the books and consider some of the odd print shop orders paid for by a chartered banker."

It didn't work. Forbes made no move to draw on Longarm as Longarm had both hands that far from his own gun.

Forbes licked his lips and meekly asked, "Isn't there some way we can settle this between ourselves, Longarm? Bank examiners can be so picky, once they start going over your books."

Longarm finished lighting the cheroot, shook out the

match and said, "I sure hope so. I've been wondering why an honest banker following safe savings and loans procedure would take such chances. But let's not worry about all that. The banking commission will doubtless know more about it in times to come. Are you figuring on still being in town when they go over your books, pard?"

The banker's comely Mex wife snapped, "*Pendejo chingado*! I told you so!" as she got to her feet and flounced inside to start packing. Longarm felt no call to translate her words as "Fucking asshole."

He said, "This newspaper pal of mine was sure glad I corrected an earlier story before it went to press. Come next week his paper will offer a full account of the whole sorry mess, naming names and fixing the blame where it belongs. Judith Morrison is going to feel mighty dumb. But seeing she was only a tool inspired by her banker and an older neighbor's clever manipulations, she'll likely live it down."

He took a drag, smiled down at Marmion and told her, "If I was you I reckon I'd sell off my stock and get on back to Texas before that *Santa Fe Weekly Democrat* gets to the general store at Last Chance, Miss Marmion."

Clora hooked a possessive arm through Longarm's as she sweetly offered to buy Double W stock at a dollar a head, seeing the two of them had so much in common.

Marmion rose to her feet, raised a hand, then dropped it as Clora stepped clear of Longarm with an expectant smile.

Marmion stared down between herself and Longarm as she sighed and said, "I thought . . . it meant something to you, Custis."

His voice was gentle as he softly replied, "It did, 'til I figured out what was going on, Miss Marmion. If it's any comfort, I'll never forget your . . . raspberry perfume."

"Am I under arrest?" she asked.

He shook his head and said, "Ain't got nothing federal on you I could hope to make stick. Do us both a favor and be on your way before anyone asks me to investigate your murder."

She ran into the house with her hands to her face.

Longarm told Clora, "Well, you said you wanted to be in on the endgame and I reckon the game's ended, here."

As the two of them walked arm in arm out to the street Clora asked if she could come back to the hotel with him and watch him pack. He told her, "When the game's ended it's best for everyone to get up from the table and count their winnings later. I'll walk you to your own mount's stable and see you off, if you want."

She said that wasn't what she wanted. She swung him around and kissed him. Then she strode off down the walk, not looking back. Longarm watched her trim figure receding from his life, shrugged and told himself not to call after her. He wanted to. But he knew he'd regret losing the chance to quit whilst he was ahead.

He moped back to his hotel, checked out and rode Dancer back to where he'd bought her. He didn't get all his money back. But it would have cost more to hire her for that many days. Patting her muzzle one last time, he moped over to the station with his McClellen, checked it through to Denver, and went out on the rear platform where it was cooler to wait for his train. He knew he faced a long ride alone up to Denver, a lot of it after dark, where you didn't get to watch the scenery and he knew he was likely to regret having passed on that last offer from a little brown-haired gal before the night was over.

But that was the way things had to be unless a man wanted to settle down and get it every night until it commenced to feel like a chore. So there was just no way that never hurt, one way or the other.

Then a red cap deposited a saratoga trunk and a redhead wearing a straw boater and a well-filled-out travel duster on the platform and ran off on her with his tip. She looked more confused than upset as Longarm rose to doff his hat to her and say, "Your servant, ma'am, if you'll allow me to help you with that baggage when our train pulls in."

She demurred that they'd never been properly introduced. So Longarm introduced himself, knowing that no
matter how things turned out, it wasn't likely to feel like a
chore.

Watch for

LONGARM AND THE PAIUTE INDIAN WAR

the 317th novel in the exciting LONGARM series
from Jove

Coming in April!

Explore the exciting Old West with one of the men who made it wild!

AVAILABLE WHEREVER BOOKS ARE SOLD OR AT WWW.PENGUIN.COM

(Ad # B112)

LONGARM

AND THE DEADLY DEAD MAN

**IN THIS GIANT-SIZED ADVENTURE,
AN OUTLAW LEARNS THAT HE'S
SAFER IN HIS GRAVE THAN
FACING AN AVENGING ANGEL
NAMED LONGARM.**

0-515-13547-X

FROM **TOM CALHOUN**

THE TEXAS
BOUNTY HUNTER SERIES
FEATURING RELENTLESS MANHUNTER
J.T. LAW

TEXAS TRACKER:
JUSTICE IN BIG SPRINGS
0-515-13850-9

TEXAS TRACKER:
SHADOW IN AUSTIN
0-515-13898-3

J. R. ROBERTS
THE GUNSMITH